'Are you mad?' she whispered.

His mouth was a hard, unremitting slash in the moonlight. 'Are you going to come with me quietly?'

'I'm not coming anywhere with you!'

He gave her a look of quietly controlled rage. 'Oh, I think so, Scarlett. A word with my wife. In private.'

'You *are* mad!' she responded in disbelief. 'I'm getting married to someone else! The divorce papers are through!'

He shook his head. 'On the contrary. You've jumped the gun a little, my dear. The divorce papers are *not* complete. The decree nisi is through—but the absolute isn't due for another five weeks. So legally, at least, you are still my wife, and I have a proposition to put to you. Now, are you coming quietly or not?'

Sharon Kendrick was born in West London and has had *heaps* of jobs which include photography, nursing, driving an ambulance across the Australian desert and cooking her way around Europe in a converted double-decker bus! Without a doubt, writing is the best job she has ever had and when she's not dreaming up new heroes (some of which are based on her doctor husband!), she likes cooking, reading, theatre, drinking wine, listening to American west coast music and talking to her two children, Celia and Patrick.

UNTAMED LOVER

BY
SHARON KENDRICK

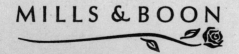

MILLS & BOON

To the inspirationally urbane Nick Foreman
and the multi-talented Wendy Sainsbury

*MILLS & BOON and the Rose Device
are trademarks of the publisher.
Harlequin Mills & Boon Limited,
Eton House, 18-24 Paradise Road, Richmond, Surrey TW9 1SR*

© Sharon Kendrick 1996

ISBN 0 263 79473 3

*Set in Times Roman 11 on 12 pt.
01-9605-46510 C1*

Made and printed in Great Britain

CHAPTER ONE

'I DON'T particularly want to talk about Liam,' said Scarlett, forcing her voice to be cool only with a monumental effort. She pulled on a black silk stocking. 'And certainly not on the night when I'm getting engaged to someone else.'

'Don't you?' taunted Camilla softly. 'But you were thinking about him just now, weren't you? I could tell by the look on your face.'

Scarlett fixed a look of nonchalant bemusement onto her face; it was a familiar look and one which she had perfected—the bright mask she hid behind. Then she outstared Camilla—whom she'd known since they were three years old—just daring her to challenge her. 'Thinking about *Liam*?' she queried, even managing a throaty note of amusement. 'Are you crazy?'

'No, but you were. Crazy to—'

Scarlett had had enough. 'Drop it, won't you, Camilla? And *do* leave me in peace to get dressed—otherwise I'm going to be late for my own party.'

To her immense relief Camilla disappeared, and after she'd closed the door behind her Scarlett looked down at her hands, to discover that they were trembling. Could the very mention of his name still do *that* to her?

'*Damn* Liam Rouse!' she said huskily. '*Damn* him!'

She reached up and pulled her dress off the hanger. Outrageous, she thought as she stood in the clinging black basque looking at the brand-new gown. The perfect winter party dress—a long-sleeved, figure-hugging black velvet sheath, with a flirty and flouncy little overskirt in gold-spangled black tulle. The black echoed the darkness of her hair, and the gold of the spangles reflected the strange gold gleam of her eyes. Not her usual style at all.

She slithered into it and stood in front of the full-length mirror. I don't look like me at all, she thought as she gazed back at the strangely glamorous and seductive creature. Even her hair looked completely different. Normally stubbornly straight, it usually spilled to just below her shoulders, but tonight it had been fashioned into great swirling waves by the village hairdresser. Beneath the heavy fringe the unusual clear amber, almost gold of her eyes glinted back at her.

I'd better go down and find Henry, she thought, when a movement from outside the uncurtained windows distracted her. Scarlett screwed her eyes up as she stared out into the blackness of the night at the sweeping grounds of Seymour House, her eyes lingering last on the massive oak, its bare branches heavy with snow. As she watched she thought she saw a shadow shift, and her heart accelerated with natural fear.

Was that a *man* standing there—as still and watchful as the tree itself?

Scarlett blinked and looked again, to see nothing but emptiness. There was no one there—of *course* there wasn't! Who in their right mind would be standing under an oak tree on the coldest night of the year?

Remonstrating with herself for her jumpiness and her groundless fears, she left the bedroom and swept down the magnificent staircase to the entrance hall, where Henry, her fiancé, his already thinning caramel-coloured hair gleaming under the light from the chandelier, was just giving the butler his overcoat.

He looked up as she approached, and scratched the end of his nose as he often did in moments of—for him—extreme emotion.

I wish he wouldn't *do* that with his nose, thought Scarlett, immediately feeling disloyal as she did so. She widened her lips in a smile. 'Hello, Henry!' she said brightly.

'Good evening, Scarlett.' He cleared his throat, as if he was about to make a speech. 'I must say, my dear, that the gown you're wearing looks very—fetching.'

'It fetched an exorbitant price,' remarked Scarlett. 'I can tell you that much!'

Henry frowned. 'Not exactly the most gracious way to receive a compliment, Scarlett.'

Scarlett sighed. 'Sorry. It's just that you don't usually make them.'

'Meaning that I should, I suppose?'

Meaning that she was surprised that Henry was going all romantic on her, when they both knew that romance did not figure very highly in their particular relationship. 'No, of course not. Oh, Henry—don't let's quarrel. Especially not tonight.'

'No.' Henry stared down at her. 'Speaking of which... Come with me,' he said suddenly, and took her by the hand.

'Why?'

'You'll see,' he said mysteriously.

He didn't say another word until he'd led her out onto the terrace, where the iridescent outline of an enormous moon tempted them with her promise.

Once there, he looked about, as though checking that the coast was clear, then he smiled as he put his hand in his pocket and drew out a small turquoise box, elaborately tied with a white ribbon.

Scarlett shivered.

'Well? Aren't you wondering what's in here?' he asked teasingly.

Scarlett played the game. She was good at playing games. 'Tell me!'

Henry waggled a finger at her. 'Patience! Patience!' And he flipped the top off to reveal a mammoth diamond solitaire. It captured every ray of the moonlight and glittered there in all its cold, cold beauty.

As if she were observing it happening to someone else, Scarlett watched while Henry slipped the solitaire onto her left ring finger, but the ring was slightly too large, and the weighty stone slid underneath her finger, leaving just the plain gold band visible—like a wedding band...

Scarlett shivered again.

'Don't worry,' said Henry easily. 'I can have it altered first thing. I wanted it to be a surprise.'

'It's—absolutely beautiful,' said Scarlett, slightly awestruck.

'Why, thank you!' And Henry pulled her into his arms and bent his head to kiss her.

It was just unfortunate that at precisely that moment Scarlett turned her head, certain that she'd heard a noise behind her, so that Henry missed her mouth completely and his kiss ended up on her left cheek.

He gave a self-conscious laugh, and planted a quick kiss on her mouth before drawing away. 'Don't worry, old girl,' he said gruffly. 'I won't bother you too much about that sort of thing.' He lowered his voice. 'Messy, overrated business, in my opinion. Though, of course, we'll have to think about producing an heir at some point.'

Scarlett stared at him, the full impact of his words hitting her like a dull blow. 'That sort of thing.' 'Messy, overrated business.' She swallowed. Sex with Henry. It was a subject she had found only too easy to ignore up until now. Because sex with anyone other than Liam was simply unimaginable. But after she and Henry were married...

'Don't worry about it,' said Henry quickly. 'I told you—I shan't be a demanding sort of husband. Now—why don't we go inside, find ourselves a glass of champagne and start showing your ring off?'

Feeling slightly ill, Scarlett allowed him to lead her back inside, and the first person they saw was her stepfather.

'Evening, Sir Humphrey!' said Henry enthusiastically. 'Just bought the lady a bauble!'

'Let's see!' Sir Humphrey peered down at Scarlett's ring. 'Nice size, Henry! Good investment. Where d'you get it?'

'Tiffany's, actually.' Henry beamed. 'As you suggested, Sir Humphrey.'

'Good choice!' said Sir Humphrey, and pumped Henry's hand approvingly.

'Like it, Scarlett?'

'Adore it!' she answered lightly as she looked up at her stepfather.

How *old* he was looking tonight, she thought suddenly. How lined his face seemed. His business, she knew, was in trouble. Although nothing had been said to her directly, she'd heard faint whispers that his company was not doing as well as it could be. The cold fingers of the recession had touched the Seymours too.

Even Scarlett had noticed of late that the roof of Seymour House was in need of repair. It was easy to see where economies *could* be made—Sir Humphrey was paying out far more on staff than he needed to, for example. But then again, since gaining his knighthood he had developed a certain sense of *noblesse oblige*. There wasn't any way that he would dream of getting rid of staff. After all, what *would* the neighbours say?

Not for the first time, Scarlett wondered why her stepfather was going to all the expense of having a huge engagement party followed by a lavish wedding. When she'd asked him his reply had been quite emphatic.

'Got to do things properly, Scarlett,' he'd answered briskly.

Scarlett had wanted to wait until things started picking up a bit—weddings were *so* expensive—but Sir Humphrey had been adamant that it should take place as soon as possible.

'I want to see you happy and settled,' he'd said, a nerve twitching in the side of his cheek.

And Scarlett had allowed her mother—who doted on Sir Humphrey and would have done anything to fall in with his wishes—to gently persuade her to go ahead with the wedding.

Scarlett fastened her social smile to her lips as the guests started arriving in earnest. Wraps and jackets were pulled off to reveal shimmering dresses in jewel-bright colours, complemented by the sombre formality of the men's black dinner jackets. The aristocracy were at play, and soon the party was in full swing.

First there was a supper of fresh salmon. Raspberries and strawberries were served for pudding, along with big bowls of golden clotted cream, then cheese platters, dotted with exotic fruits.

There was to be no engagement cake, nor speeches—it was too close to the wedding for that—but the large dining-room was cleared for dancing, and as Henry took Scarlett into his arms to start the dancing the guests began to applaud. It was a slow number, and they drifted around the floor.

'Everything seems to be going splendidly.' He smiled contentedly as they moved in time to the music.

Her golden eyes sparked back. 'Don't speak too soon—I'll probably step on your toes in a minute!'

'Are you *never* serious?' he laughed.

'Never!' She smiled back. She'd learnt her lesson about being serious. If you were serious about things you got your heart broken; if you were flippant—you survived.

He dropped his hands from her waist as the music came to an end. 'Look—your father is beckoning me. I'd better go and see what it is he wants. Go and circulate, darling.'

Scarlett watched him go, feeling suddenly deflated as she looked around the room at all the glittering dancers, a lot of whom were strangers to her. I feel as if I'm on the outside looking in, she thought suddenly. As though I don't belong here. The way I've always felt in this house. The child with its nose pressed up against the lighted shop window.

Oh, stop being so *ridiculous*, she remonstrated with herself silently as she left the room and slipped quietly out onto the terrace for a breath of fresh air. That champagne has just made me maudlin, she thought crossly as she took a deep breath and inhaled the sweet scent of the winter-flowering jasmine.

She stood, silent and spellbound, oblivious to the cold as she gazed at the beautiful vista before her.

The snow-covered grass was glitteringly silver, and high up in the sky the moon looked like a brilliant white discus, hurled there by some Olympian athlete, and as she watched a cloud obscured it completely.

Scarlett's eyes narrowed as they accustomed themselves to the dimmer light, and she blinked as she saw a man's figure standing at one end of the terrace. He was staring at her.

She felt her heart pound in shock as she registered the immense height of him, the formidable breadth of his shoulders. She shook her head in horror, as if expecting him just to disappear. But he did not disappear. Instead he began to walk towards her with a confident and cat-like stealth.

Scarlett blanched as the man grew closer. Her eyes took in the beautifully sculpted planes and angles of his face, the harsh slash of his mouth and the proud line of his jaw.

He was taller than anyone else at the party, and his shoulders would have put deep despair into the heart of any rugby scrum. His hair was black, as black as Scarlett's, and his eyes, which she knew so well were blue, also looked black tonight. And his heart, she thought bitterly. He has a black heart too. The beautiful mouth was curved and twisted into its customary derisory smile as his eyes met Scarlett's—and never left them.

For a second she shook her head a little, as if she had manufactured the image of Liam Rouse. For surely this could not be Liam—this man whose formal black jacket would have knocked spots off everyone else's in the room? Surely not Liam—in a silk shirt as white as a soap-powder commercial, with a black bow-tie knotted around his elegant neck? Liam's long legs would surely never have allowed themselves to be encased in the beautifully cut black trousers. Liam wore jeans. Nothing but jeans.

She stared up at him as he towered over her, momentarily shocked into disbelieving speechlessness. She saw his eyes glittering, like some living metal, and she had to reach out to grasp the balustrade which ran round the terrace.

Her heart pounded with unwilling excitement, and her mouth dried. It simply wasn't fair, she thought desperately. He shouldn't, *shouldn't* still have this effect on her. Not after all this time. 'Liam!' she gasped as the vision of the man she had not seen for almost ten years swam in front of her eyes. And then she found herself saying inanely, 'Is it really you?'

He gave a small, cynical smile. 'Judge for yourself,' came the deeply drawled reply, and totally without warning he pulled her into his arms and bent his head to kiss her.

At first she was so shocked by what was happening that she simply stood motionless in his arms, while his mouth claimed hers with arrogant possession.

And Liam's kisses were like no others . . .

Oh, no! she thought helplessly, but nonetheless swayed against him as his mouth drove down on hers, her body quivering with shock as she realised just how blatantly he was kissing her. For his kiss was as deep and as insistent and intimate as if he were lying naked on top of her and actually making love to her.

He pulled her closer, then even closer... And to her absolute horror Scarlett found herself responding to him, her body starting to tingle and melt into the hard, muscle-packed frame which she had once known so intimately.

He knew so well what pleased her, she thought helplessly. She felt him lick a tiny circle around the inside of her mouth, and as she felt her breasts swelling and hardening in response she realised just what was happening to her. She wrenched herself out of his embrace, and he gave a low, mocking laugh.

'Well?' he said arrogantly. 'Was that real enough for you? Or do I kiss like a ghost?'

She fought to get her breath back. 'You kiss like the devil that you are!' she fired back. 'Now, get off our land, before I have you thrown off!'

'Oh, Scarlett,' he said mockingly. 'No wifely concern? No, "Darling, where have you been all these long years?"'

Scarlett stared into the face of the stranger who was as familiar to her as breathing—the man who had broken her heart into a million tiny pieces. 'I don't care *where* you've been,' she retorted angrily. 'You walked off and left me ten years ago without a word. Well, that was fine. But you're history, Liam. And now I'm going inside to call the police to get you off our property—unless you'd like to go now, and quietly?'

He gave a short, completely humourless laugh and reached out to catch her wrist in an uncompromising hold. 'Oh, but that's where you're wrong,' he contradicted her, his voice as hard and as unmalleable as steel. 'I'm not going anywhere—not until I've got what I came for.'

She heard the unswerving determination in the deep voice, and a deep foreboding chilled her. Liam at twenty had been pretty formidable. Liam ten years on was something else!

In a minute she would wake up from this nightmare, but until she did she might as well enter into this crazy conversation. 'What the hell are you talking about? What have you come for?' But her voice wavered just a little as she asked the question.

His eyes fastened with deliberate intent on the crimson gleam of her quivering mouth, and she saw his eyes briefly darken. 'Why, you, of course, Scarlett. Didn't you realise? I've come for you.'

'Are you mad?' she whispered.

His mouth was a hard, unremitting slash in the moonlight. 'Are you going to come with me quietly?'

'I'm not coming anywhere with you!'

He gave her a look of quietly controlled rage. 'Oh, I think so, Scarlett. A word with my wife. In private.'

'You *are* mad!' she responded in disbelief. 'I'm getting married to someone else! The divorce papers are through!'

He shook his head. 'On the contrary. You've jumped the gun a little, my dear. The divorce papers are *not* complete. Admittedly, the decree nisi is through—but the absolute isn't due for another five weeks.' He gave a cold and cynical smile. 'So legally, at least, you are still my wife, and I have a proposition to put to you. Now, are you coming quietly or not?' he repeated.

The craziness of the last few minutes crystallised into one incredible and jarring fact.

Liam was back!

She found her voice again. '*Coming*? With you? You *must* be kidding! The last person on earth I'd ever go with is you—you no-good, low-down, rotten—!'

Again, he gave that cool, faintly cynical smile.

'Oh, Scarlett,' he said, shaking his head at her as he caught her wrist in a vice-like grip. 'I should have known that you'd be awkward.'

'Let go of me!' she ordered. 'Or I'll scream the place down.'

'Oh, dear,' he murmured, almost conversationally. 'I was hoping that we might be able to do this in a civilised manner. But then, I'd forgotten that legendary temper of yours.'

She tried to struggle, but it was no good. Even using her one free hand to flail at that impossibly hard chest was useless, and he bent down to scoop her underneath her knees and toss her over his shoulder, her head dangling down his back and his hand clasped possessively over the bare flesh of the backs of her thighs which lay above the line of her stocking-tops. He stroked one thigh with a long, lazy finger.

'Mmm!' he murmured, in a voice soft with sexual promise. '*Nice!*'

And then something unbelievable happened.

For one fleeting and betraying moment a spark of dormant humour bubbled up from deep within her, and somehow that ability of his to make her smile was in its own way far more damaging than his ability to wring a physical response from her. He was certainly the most unconventional man she'd ever met in her life! And she was back in his arms! But she quelled the betraying spark immediately as she remembered just what he'd done.

Liam had left her at the lowest point in her life, and for that she would never forgive him. 'I hate you,' she muttered into his back as he walked towards the drive.

'And the feeling,' he said, in a strangely bitter voice, 'is entirely mutual.'

CHAPTER TWO

'PUT me down!' Scarlett shrieked into the cold white night, but Liam completely ignored her and carried on calmly walking through the snow towards a low black car which was parked at the end of the driveway.

Surely someone would see them go? And think it odd that this towering dark man was carrying the hostess over his shoulder through the snow. Where the hell was Henry, or her stepfather? 'Put me down, or I'll scream!'

'Scream and I'll have to kiss you quiet!' he threatened savagely.

And, because she didn't trust herself to risk *that*, Scarlett hastily closed the mouth which she had opened to give him the full benefit of her loudest, most ear-piercing shriek, right next to his ear.

He reached the car and pulled open the driver's door, only to lift her over onto the passenger seat and snap her seatbelt shut. Then, with an agility remarkable for such a tall man, he slid his long legs into the seat next to her, belted himself in and started up the powerful engine, which gave a low, throaty roar as the car shot off.

She pulled at the lock, but it wouldn't budge.

'We're doing fifty, and that door is safety-primed not to open while the car is in motion, so you might as well sit back and enjoy the ride.'

This could not be happening to her. In a minute she would be back at the party, in Henry's safe and undemanding arms.

'Stop this car at once!'

'No.'

'Where are you taking me?'

'You'll see,' came the implacable reply.

She knew that determined set of his mouth from old—knew that it signalled the inexorable side of his nature. And she sat back in a daze against the soft leather of the seat before her senses began to return, and with them her temper.

'This is kidnap, you do realise that?'

'Is it? A court might see it differently—a husband making a last-minute stab at reconciliation...'

Quite without warning her heart gave a sudden lurch as she remembered the nights she'd spent sobbing into her pillow, not really believing that he had walked out on her for good. Oh, the black, heartless devil! 'But Liam,' she said coldly, 'you seem to have missed the whole point of the party which you gatecrashed. I'm going to be married in five weeks' time. To Henry.'

'Are you?' he queried silkily.

'Yes, I am!' But Scarlett found herself shivering at his deep, dark voice—hating herself for the little frisson of awareness which traced sensuous fingers up the entire length of her spine. Just what was it about this particular man which sent her senses into overdrive? 'Where are you taking me?' she demanded again, hearing her own tame question with appalled disbelief. Why wasn't she screaming the place down?

Because it wouldn't do her any good; she knew that. He was too strong to resist. And not just physically either.

He didn't answer, just gave her a brief sideways glance—in time to see the tremble that convulsed her upper body. 'You're cold,' he remarked, and put out a strong brown hand to turn the heating up.

'Of course I'm cold!' she returned. 'It's the middle of winter, it's snowing, and I'm wearing very thin clothes.'

'And very little underwear, from what I saw,' he grated. 'You never used to wear such sexy little bits of nonsense when you were married to me! But then I don't really remember you wearing much underwear at all. The problem *we* had, as I recall, was keeping it *on*.'

Scarlett's mouth fell wide open as she turned to look at him in disbelieving shock. 'What was that you said?'

'You heard.'

'You were spying on me!' she realised in horror. 'As I was standing in front of the window I *knew* that someone was out there, watching me. It was you!'

'Who did you think it would be?' he mocked. 'Was the floor show for dear Henry? Hoping to inspire a little passion in him, were you, Scarlett?

Let's hope for your sake that he makes love more
accurately than he kisses.'

'Why, you—!' Her hand went up automatically.

'Don't even think of it,' his cold voice rang out.
'I'm driving, remember?'

'You couldn't stop me if I wanted to!' she
taunted.

'Couldn't I?' he said quietly. 'I could stop this
car right now and quieten you down very effec-
tively, Scarlett—and I'm sure you don't need to ask
me how.'

Her hand fell to her lap, her cheeks flushed pink
in the darkness. This was madness! Sheer madness.
Liam was *kidnapping* her, for God's sake, and she
was just sitting back in her seat like a lemon and
letting him!

'You just can't *do* this to me!' she protested.

'I just did.'

'Haven't you got any consideration for other
people? My stepfather will be worried sick about
me.'

'He'll survive,' he said coldly.

'He'll call the police,' she said, equally coldly.

'I don't doubt it.'

'And you'll be arrested. Slung into jail.' She
heard her voice rising sharply. 'Though it probably
won't be the first time, will it, Liam?'

She saw the merest glimmer of amusement hover
around a mouth that was far too delectable for its
own good. 'You think I've done time?' he queried,
almost casually.

'*Nothing* would surprise me about you!' she said, with feeling.

'Well, that's good, Scarlett,' he drawled. 'Never underestimate your opponent—that's the first ground rule for battle.'

She felt sadness mixed with fury. They were battling now; they had battled then. Their whole brief relationship had been a war, punctuated with wild flurries of peace in the form of their ecstatic love-making. She hunted around for the *coup de grâce* to wound him. 'Well, I'd like to know where you got the money to pay for this fancy car,' she said insultingly.

She saw his knuckles tighten for an instant on the steering wheel, but there was nothing but sardonic amusement in his voice as he spoke. 'Sorry to disappoint you, Scarlett, but your patronising Lady Bountiful act fails to impress me.'

'It used to, though,' she said bitterly. 'I thought that my classy accent turned you on. I thought you liked hob-nobbing with the gentry—almost as much as I liked slumming it with you.'

The lie sounded convincing—even to her. Let him believe that her passion for him had been the youthful experimentation of a naïve young girl, which had quickly faded. Never let him know that he had been the love of her life, the man with whom she had constantly found herself comparing other men. And hadn't the other men always come up lacking? Wasn't that why she'd agreed to an eminently 'suitable' marriage to Henry—because she'd given up looking for love?

'Slumming, huh?' The deep voice was clinical, detached... The old Liam would have exploded with anger at the jibe, stopped whatever he was doing and taken her into his arms with a ruthless passion which would have had her denying anything he'd wanted her to deny.

But this Liam—this stranger in the suit—he merely reached out and pushed a cassette into the tape deck, and music filled the car.

Scarlett could have screamed as the violently passionate strains of the love-scene from *Carmen* pierced the air with frighteningly sweet sensuality. But short of actually putting her fingers in her ears, there wasn't a lot she could do to blot the sound out. Instead, she stared fixedly ahead at the empty road. When had he learnt to like opera? she wondered with a sudden bitterness.

She realised with a sudden shock that she had never seen him drive before either. During their lamentably brief and ill-fated marriage they had been desperately short of money—and Liam had stubbornly refused to accept any hand-outs from her stepfather. Which was why they'd lived in the small, dingy flat over the café, where the smell of cabbage had drifted upwards and seemed to permeate even their clothes and their skin. And where Scarlett would play at being a housewife while Liam went out to his labouring job each morning.

She had to think clearly. Liam was back, but there was a limit to how far even he would go. What was he planning? And why, for goodness' sake, was she just accepting this dramatic seizure, as though it was inevitable? As though, with him around, she had no conscious will of her own?

Drawing her shoulders back, she sat up straight in her seat and forced herself to take note of land-marks as the snow-clothed countryside flashed by. Her heart started hammering as she recognised the village as they drove quietly through it and circum-navigated the iced-over village pond.

The road out of it was narrow, winding. She closed her eyes quickly, not daring to open them again, although she knew exactly what she would see if she did. To her left she would see a dramatic line of horse-chestnuts, like scarecrows of the gods, waving their bare black arms against the heavy, snow-laden sky.

How *could* he have done? she wondered with helpless bitterness. To have brought her here...

'Afraid to look, Scarlett?' mocked the deep voice beside her, and she fluttered open her eyelids in de-fiance, still not believing it to be true. Her heart was sinking, yet at the same time it started to hammer with some shameful excitement as the car drew up in front of the small cottage.

As he turned the engine off she released her seatbelt and turned on him, her long nails instinc-tively forming cat-like talons which attempted to scrabble at his face. But he fended them off as a tiger would swat a butterfly, his big, strong hands closing decisively over hers.

There was a cold, cruel smile on his face as he watched her lips part automatically as their skin made contact. 'Fight me all you like, Scarlett—but why don't we get horizontal first?' he said insultingly. But before she could retaliate he had unbuckled his seatbelt, stepped out of the car, had walked around to her side and was doing the same for her.

'Take me home at once!' she said flatly. 'If you do that, and leave me alone, I'll let the whole matter drop.'

'Not even a little bit curious, Scarlett, to know what your dear husband has been doing for all these years?'

'Not in the least.' Her eyes deliberately swept down every inch of the superbly cut and outrageously expensive suit. 'Something underhand, I shouldn't doubt—judging from the money you're obviously throwing around.'

'You think so?' he asked softly.

Hurt him, urged an inner voice. Hurt him badly, as he hurt you. She gave him a supercilious little smile. 'How *did* you make your money, then, Liam?' she said patronisingly. 'Labouring?'

'But I thought you liked all that kind of thing, sweetheart?' he drawled. 'Your bit of *rough*,' he added with insulting emphasis.

She felt all the blood drain from her face. 'Why, you arrogant blackguard!' she gasped out. Her eyes hardened to match the coldness in his. 'Take me home, Liam!'

Soft snowflakes were fluttering onto the jet hair which the light breeze ruffled as he shook his head. 'Not yet. I want to talk to you,' he said, with the kind of steely emphasis used by a man not used to taking no for an answer.

'See my solicitor.'

'What's the matter, Scarlett?' he mocked. 'Afraid to go inside? Does the past repulse you so much?'

As he drew her attention to the cottage she gave him her haughtiest look, narrowing her eyes so that he would be unable to read any of the nostalgic pain in her eyes. Not here, anywhere but here, where her love for him had been born. It had been in there—in that cottage—that she'd given herself to him one summer afternoon.

On a dusty floor he had slowly bared her flesh, had kissed her and possessed her with such exquisite sweetness. She had cried afterwards, salty tears of grateful joy sliding into his shoulders and down his chest. But even as the shudders had died away in his own body she had felt his anger. As though he had already sensed the repercussions of that sweet, wild mating...

'Quite frankly, I can hardly remember the place,' she lied frostily. 'But, as you know, my stepfather owns it. So, as well as abduction we can add trespassing to your charge-sheet.'

He gave a short, abrasive laugh. 'I think not,' he said arrogantly. 'Come inside, Scarlett. I told you—we need to talk, and it's too cold to stay out here.'

He pulled her out of the car, not roughly, but with that gentle strength which had always been at the heart of his lovemaking. And for one bizarre moment of insanity Scarlett had to steel herself not to sink into those powerful arms.

'I'll never forgive you for this!' she said fervently as he guided her towards the door and unlocked it.

'That is purely academic.' The handsome face was impassive, as if he didn't care one way or the other.

Scarlett walked in, and her mouth fell open in surprise. In her mind's eye she had imagined that the cottage would look exactly the same—neglected and run-down, bare and dilapidated—but to her astonishment someone had done the place up. And had done it up beautifully too.

The floorboards had been properly waxed to a deep shine, and Persian rugs in vibrant hues of sapphire and turquoise silk were scattered around. The walls had been recently covered in a pale wash and hung with several superb watercolours. Soft and pale modern furniture provided the seating. Someone had put central heating in too. Whoever had decorated had exquisite taste, and it had nothing of her parents' rather predictable penchant for old-fashioned polished mahogany.

'Who owns this?' asked Scarlett suddenly.

'I do.'

'I don't believe you!' But her denial was merely automatic; his words had held the unmistakable ring of truth.

'That is, of course, your prerogative,' he said coolly.

Scarlett was growing more confused by the moment. 'But my stepfather would never sell it—certainly not to *you*!'

'So sure?' A kind of smile curved the corners of his lips upwards, though his blue eyes stayed as cold as the temperature outside, and something in the oddly confident look on his face filled her with a strange kind of dread. Of course her stepfather wouldn't have sold him the cottage! Why on earth would he have had any dealings with a man he detested almost as much as she did?

'Sit down, Scarlett, while I light the fire. Coffee? Or perhaps you'd prefer something stronger?'

This was crazy! Any minute now and they'd be discussing politics—and here, of all places! She needed to get out—before the past, with its shockingly poignant memories, started that aching in her heart all over again. 'I want *out*, that's what I want—back to my party! You said you wanted to talk, Liam—then start talking. I'll give you five minutes.'

'We need some heat first.' And he crouched down to start the fire. Flames leapt up and licked realistically at logs, and suddenly the room looked deceptively and cloyingly homely. Scarlett sat down on one of the squashy leather sofas, feeling as though her whole world had tipped upside-down, her reality totally distorted as she watched him pour brandy into two glasses and put them both onto a small table which sat in front of the sofa.

She glanced at her watch. It was approaching eleven. 'I can't wait for my stepfather to get here,' she said calmly.

'But not Henry?'

Henry? Scarlett stared at the hands which were clasped in her lap, wondering why she'd made the Freudian omission of neglecting to use Henry's name. She looked up, and her eyes burned a golden fire as she met his steady blue stare. 'Henry will take you to pieces. You can't just walk into my house and carry me off against my will—you bloody great brute!'

'But I just did,' he pointed out.

'If you wanted to speak to me didn't it occur to you to just pick the phone up, like anyone else would have done, and ask to meet me?'

He gave her a coldly mocking smile. 'And would you have agreed to meet me?'

'What do *you* think?'

'Well, then—I rest my case.' And he lifted his glass to her in mock toast. 'What shall we drink to?' he asked conversationally.

'How about divorce?'

'So cruel,' he remonstrated mockingly. 'And yet, really *I* am the injured party—wouldn't you say? After all, I was the one you trapped into marriage in the first place, wasn't I?'

'I didn't . . .' But her words of denial died away. Because wasn't he right, in a way? She *had* trapped him. She had wanted him, and had lured him with all calculation of the spoilt child she'd been at the time. But she had loved him, or so she'd thought.

And oh, how she'd paid a hundredfold for her youthful desire for Liam Rouse.

She watched as he slid down onto the squashy sofa opposite hers, the long black-trousered legs spread out in front of him.

Lord, but he looked good, she thought reluctantly. Still the same firmly packed muscular body, without a scrap of fat on it. The same broad chest, narrow hips and long, powerful thighs. But there was a change in him too.

She had known Liam in the very first flush of manhood, his virility untempered by anything other than need. But now... Now there was an element of rigid self-control about him, a steely determination—it was easy to see in the unperturbed watchfulness on that harshly handsome face, and even easier to read in those cold, blue eyes which unsmilingly underwent her scrutiny.

She took a deep breath and looked at him steadily, wanting to know what had turned Liam from that untamed and beautiful lover into this urbane and sophisticated man who now sat before her.

'Have you been in England all this time?'

His mouth twisted in a parody of a smile. 'Why?' he mocked softly. 'Did you miss me?'

More than he would ever know. 'I missed you like the proverbial hole in the head!' she shot back archly.

'But I bet you missed my body, Scarlett?' he murmured with ruthless accuracy. 'Mmm?'

To her horror, just the thought of his body in the context to which he was referring was enough to produce a reaction: that familiar tug which hardened her nipples to frustrated tips which just cried out for the suckling of his moist, ravening mouth; the warm pooling sensation which culminated in a hot, hot aching at the juncture of her thighs. She shifted uncomfortably in her chair, feeling the scalding flush of shame and arousal stain her cheeks, and knew that her eyes had darkened in conjunction with his. And knew that he'd missed nothing.

'Yes,' he affirmed softly. 'You missed my body like hell, Scarlett.'

Hell was appropriate enough—the smug, arrogant devil! She took a slug of brandy and managed a chilly stare. 'How tedious you can be sometimes, Liam. Have you lost all the art of polite conversation?' She gave him a mocking little smile. 'Oh! How silly of me! I forgot, of course, that you didn't really have the skill to begin with—'

'Such condescension,' he reprimanded. 'Really, Scarlett—did no one ever tell you that's a sign of low intelligence?'

And why was it she never seemed able to get the better of him in an argument? she thought furiously. 'Go to hell!' she snapped.

'Succinct,' he murmured. 'Now, what were we talking about before you sank to playground level? You were, I believe, quizzing me about my life, weren't you?'

She should stick her nose in the air and tell him that she wasn't in the *slightest* bit interested in *anything* he'd done—so it was rather strange to find herself asking, 'Where have you been all this time?'

He sipped his own drink and put the glass back down on the table. 'First I went to Australia. Then the States. My main home is still in Australia.'

And now? she thought with a sinking heart. Even out of sight, Liam had never been entirely out of mind. Surely he wasn't planning to re-enter her life? 'So now you're back for good?' she said, voicing the fear.

'That rather depends,' he said obscurely, 'on the outcome of our talk.'

Something in the way he said it alerted alarm bells in Scarlett's head. She narrowed her eyes suspiciously. 'You'd better tell me what this is all about, Liam.'

'I told you. I have a proposition to put to you.'

Curiosity got the better of her. 'What kind of proposition?'

He gave a distinctly wolfish smile. 'I need a favour from you.'

She actually laughed aloud. 'Well, if that doesn't take the biscuit for arrogant, bare-faced cheek! You reappear after ten years and then try bargaining with me? You're not in a position to negotiate.'

'Ah, but that's where you're wrong, Scarlett,' he said, in a tone of chilling assurance. 'I always operate from a position of strength. It's a lesson I learned very early on in life.'

Something about this new Liam made her feel uneasy. The years had redefined that ridiculously primitive masculinity he'd always exuded. Oh, it was still there, but tempered beneath the cool and worldly assurance he now carried with him. And, in a way, the impact was all the greater under its new guise. The hand of steel masked beneath the velvet glove...but just as hard and as impenetrable as ever...

He had been cold and unfeeling, she thought bitterly. He had walked away without giving her a second thought—well, she was damned if she'd let him back into her life on any terms!

She studied him, feigning impartiality. 'Tell me what you're asking,' she said. 'But I haven't any money to give you,' she added insultingly.

This brought a reaction. It was so fleeting that someone who had not made a hobby out of studying his harsh features might have missed it completely. But it was there, and Scarlett saw it. Rage, in about as undiluted a form as you could get it, burned like a blazing fire in those blue eyes. Rage, which somehow—sinisterly—managed to convey some kind of threat. And as she felt her heartbeat pick up she realised that it was a sexual threat, communicated silently to her traitorous and willing body.

Then it was gone. Instead, the eyes were narrowed, ill-concealed distaste replacing rage. 'You think I need your money?' he questioned softly. 'That even if I did I would ever come crawling back to ask *you*? And I can imagine what you'd like in exchange for your money too.' His eyes glittered with censure. 'Well, I'm sorry to disappoint you, Scarlett, but I played the role of stud just once in my life—and that was once too often.'

Scarlett stared at him in horrified disbelief. He couldn't believe *that*—he just couldn't! Surely he didn't believe that it had just been the bed thing for her? He had been her entire world, her universe. For her, the sun had risen and set in Liam's eyes. She shuddered at the memory before answering him.

'While you may have the time or the inclination to sit around here discussing an episode of our lives best left forgotten—I do not.' She stared at her wristwatch pointedly. 'I have a party going on, guests waiting—so come on, out with it, Liam.'

There was the faintest upward pull at the corner of his mouth, and to her consternation she felt her cheeks flame at his silent acknowledgement of sexual innuendo.

'Get on with it!' She glared at him. 'And tell me about your *proposition*.'

'So delightfully put,' he murmured, then crossed one long leg over the other. 'Very well. We've tarried for long enough. You see, it's not your money I need, Scarlett—it's you.'

To her fury, her heart had resumed its excited little pitter-pattering. Some long-forgotten yearning deep within her flared into tentative life. She found herself swallowing. 'What did you say?' she whispered.

He smiled. 'I want you to do me a little favour, Scarlett,' he said softly.

The yearning crumbled into dust, but some glittering message which sparked at the depths of his eyes warned her not to simply ignore his statement. 'What kind of favour?'

He smiled again. He looked invincible. 'I have a big business merger going through. Contracts are about to be signed. All I need to do is put the icing on top of the cake, so to speak, so I'm holding a house party at one of my homes in Australia for my prospective business colleagues and their wives. I want everything to run like clockwork, and I need a hostess—someone who knows how to play the part to perfection—and who better than you, Scarlett?' he finished mockingly.

CHAPTER THREE

SCARLETT stared at Liam as though he had just spouted horns and a tail. She shook her head from side to side in disbelief. 'It's a preposterous suggestion! Laughable! It doesn't even deserve the dignity of an answer.'

He didn't seem in the least bit perturbed by her negative response. 'You won't do it, then?'

She nearly choked on the last of the brandy she had been drinking to gain a bit of Dutch courage. 'Of course I won't do it! I don't know how you've got the brass neck to even consider it! As if I'd endure even a minute more of your company than I have to—let alone take part in some farcical "house party" to impress your business cronies. And if I did meet any of them, I'd take great delight in telling them—'

'How great I am in bed?' he mocked softly, giving a deep laugh as he saw the colour which scorched over her pale skin.

'That was completely unnecessary, *and* below the belt!'

He raised his eyebrows infinitesimally and gave a very sexy smirk. 'I certainly hope so,' he drawled.

Scarlett gave up. His sexual innuendo she couldn't cope with—not when she was marooned out in the middle of nowhere with him. It was time to put her foot down—once and for all!

'How many times do I have to tell you? Watch my lips, Liam! I am engaged to someone else! And, just in case that's still not clear enough, watch my lips again! In five weeks' time you and I will be divorced!'

'So I take it the answer is no?' came the mocking reply.

'Have the last ten years done something to your powers of reasoning?' she demanded. 'Of course the answer's no!'

He shook his head, as though mildly irritated, nothing more. 'Oh, dear. And there was me hoping that we would be able to agree on this amicably.'

'Which just goes to show how wrong you can be!'

'Scarlett,' he drawled, 'I'm afraid that there isn't really a pleasant way to say what I'm about to say—'

'Then why bother?' she cut in.

'You'll see. Do you have any knowledge of your stepfather's affairs?'

She shot him a bewildered look. 'What are you talking about?' she demanded. 'He's always been completely faithful to my mother.'

'Not *those* kinds of affairs,' he chided. 'Heavens, Scarlett—you always did have a one-track mind. I'm talking about his business affairs.'

What on earth did Liam know about Humphrey's business affairs? 'What about them?'

'Your stepfather is teetering on the brink of bankruptcy,' he stated baldly.

There was something about the flat, unequivocal statement that had the undeniable ring of truth about it. Scarlett tried to swamp the sudden fear which rose in her throat.

'I don't believe you,' she said quietly.

There was a grim expression on his face which hardened the brilliant blue of his eyes into shards of glittering sapphire. 'Believe it,' he said flatly. 'This cottage I now own—as I do the majority of your stepfather's old estate.'

Scarlett's heart started thudding loudly. 'Liar,' she whispered.

He ignored the interruption. 'His business is in trouble and his house is mortgaged up to the hilt. And if the bank were to call in its loans, well...' He gave a sardonic smile as he paused for dramatic emphasis.

'And why should the bank want to do that?' she asked steadily. 'And what has all this got to do with you? And me?'

'It has everything to do with you and me,' he said, in the kind of hard, harsh voice which took her back years, to the twin emotions of sorrow and joy inextricably linked in her mind with Liam.

'I own the controlling interest in the bank which has allowed Humphrey to remortgage his house and finance his business. I could call in his loans tomorrow. If you force me to.'

'What are you saying?' she whispered. 'I don't understand.'

'I've told you, Scarlett. I want you to play hostess for me. Do that—just that—and I'll leave him alone.'

She looked at the hard-eyed man who sat before her, his face as unreadable as if he were playing poker. 'You big bully!' she cried. 'He's getting old—how can you possibly—?'

'Shut up,' he ground out, and she saw his pupils dilate as his temper finally snapped. 'Don't talk to me about bullying, or tactics! However misguided our brief marriage might have been there was no excuse for the way your stepfather behaved.'

Scarlett felt hot colour flare into her cheeks. She knew exactly what he was referring to. 'If it's about your mother, I made him promise to get her—'

'*You* made him promise!' he said bitterly. 'What good could a mere slip of a girl do against a man whose reputation was paramount to him? Damn him and his reputation!'

The anger was suddenly replaced with a stealthy watchfulness, which was somehow even more intimidating than the fury which had preceded it. 'Shall I tell you what your stepfather did, Scarlett?' he queried softly. 'Or do you already know?'

'He said he had found her another job...' Her voice died away as she read the contempt in his eyes.

'He was lying. You knew that there was no other job for her, didn't you?' he said coldly.

'And what was I supposed to do?' she demanded. 'Create one for her? At eighteen? Besides, I—'

'Your pride was hurt because I'd left you? Yes? So my mother deserved everything she got?'

Maybe for an instant—but no more than that. 'I always liked and respected your mother,' she said.

'Pity that *Humphrey's* response wasn't so measured,' he grated sarcastically. 'She'd done nothing but work hard for him, but not only did he sack her, he also refused to give her a reference.'

Scarlett felt a bitter pang of shame sweep over her. She didn't know whether he saw it, but he suddenly sprang to his feet, his back to her, the set of his shoulders iron-hard and rigid, his body as tightly controlled as that of an automaton. And somehow she knew that he was breaking up inside—Liam, the man who so rarely showed emotion.

She wanted suddenly, quite instinctively, to go over to him, to take him in her arms with all the freedom to touch him which she'd had during their marriage. And she knew that he would probably lash out at her if she dared try.

'What happened to her?' she asked.

The voice was calm again. Calm, cool and matter-of-fact. 'What usually happens to women without husbands in late middle-age who are forced to start over again? I gave her what money I could from the labouring you so despised. But she was forced to accept benefits from the State. It was that which galled her more than anything else—she was a proud woman,' he said, almost to himself.

'Eventually, she found herself another position, in another big house. Hard-working women of that calibre always do.' His eyes were steely. 'But it was never quite the same for her. She didn't know anyone. She was getting too old to make new friends. And, of course, I had left home. She lost her enthusiasm for life. The ingredients for catastrophe were all there—a poor diet, economies made on heating bills... She died two years later of a heart condition.'

'Oh, Liam—I'm so sorry,' said Scarlett quietly.

He turned, then, blue eyes blazing like the devil's. 'Are you?' he demanded harshly. 'Are you really, Scarlett?'

She recoiled from the bitter fury and accusation in his voice, staring up at him in utter bewilderment. 'For heaven's sake, Liam—are you blaming *me* for your mother's death? Is that what this is all about?'

'I don't know what I'm blaming you for!' he ground out. 'Maybe I'm blaming you for still wanting to do *this*—even after all this time.'

She gasped and swayed as he caught her in a brutal embrace, hauling her up from the sofa and into his arms like some stormy-eyed, marauding conqueror. And it was like the very first time he'd kissed her all over again to be desired with such dark, elemental passion.

His mouth burned as it caught hers, setting her aflame instantly. He kissed her with a fierce, demanding pressure, and he met no resistance, because for that moment she understood his need to punish her—welcomed it, almost—and she kissed him back with her own bitter reprimand, utterly discounting the fact that each was trying to inflict hurt on the other with this savage kiss, and the fact that instead all they were succeeding in doing was becoming embroiled in a hot, sexual battle which could have only one satisfactory conclusion.

He moved his mouth away from hers a fraction, to give him enough air to speak. 'Yes, you little bitch,' he whispered huskily. 'You still have the power to make me desire you like this—even though I despise myself for doing it.'

Scarlett shuddered in his arms, but even his cruel words were not enough to break the bars of this enchanting prison. Instead, she allowed him to push his hips into hers, allowed herself to feel the tantalising length of him, swollen hard with the desire he so despised.

His hand moved down her back to her buttocks, tightly encased in the black velvet of her dress, and he splayed his fingers to cup her possessively against him, giving the humourless laugh of the unwilling victor as he did so.

'Oh, yes, Scarlett. I want to rip that pretty little dress from your body,' he said thickly, and the slurred, heavy undertones of pure desire set her trembling again. 'I want to see you in your fancy stockings and suspenders. *Me*, only me—do you understand that, Scarlett? For my eyes only. And then I want to take them off, as slowly as you like.

'I want to see all that soft white flesh again. I want to bury my head in your breasts, to suckle you until you weep. I want to lie naked on top of you, inside you. I want to lose myself deep within you. Is that what you want? Do you want that too, my little temptress, Scarlett?'

Like an unwilling intruder she heard her treacherous little voice make a gasping little sound of assent. There was only this. Only them. How right it felt to be wrapped in Liam's strong embrace again, to feel the hunger building up between them. Only this man could turn her into some frantic, wild, sensual being. Only Liam. Henry had never once...

As her fiancé's name crept into her thoughts it was like being doused with ice-cold water. Her eyes snapped open as she prepared to see the passion written all over Liam's face, but she was too late. He had felt her mental withdrawal instantly. The blue eyes had hooded over; his stare was nothing but cool and thoughtful. Only the darkness of his mouth gave evidence of what had just happened, the bruised fullness of his bottom lip a glaring testimony to the intensity of their shared kisses.

Scarlett was shamefully aware of the singing of the blood in her throbbing and swollen breasts. She saw his eyes flicker there briefly, saw the flare of predatory satisfaction light the blue eyes. And she knew that any stumbling protestations about that kiss would rightfully earn her nothing but his scorn and derision. Because you could have stopped him, taunted the voice of her conscience. And what is more you *should* have stopped him.

But could she have? Surely to have tried to stop something which had briefly filled her with the most delicious longing would have been about as futile as King Canute trying to hold back the tide?

What could she do other than pretend nothing had happened?

She stared at him quite calmly, her body now almost back to normal. 'You aren't serious about me coming to Australia, are you, Liam? Not really?'

'Oh, but that's where you're wrong. I am. Deadly serious.'

She swallowed. 'And the deal is that if I refuse you will call in my stepfather's loans?'

'You've got it in one.'

'You bastard,' she said softly. 'And what do I tell Henry?'

He shrugged. 'No need to tell him anything too explicit,' he mocked, his eyes sparkling as they moved deliberately to her swollen breasts, and the temptation to slap his face was almost over-whelming. But violence would only add to this siz-zling cauldron of emotions.

'You'll think of something, Scarlett. An enter-prising young woman like you. Write him a note telling him you'll be away for a fortnight at most. Imply that you're shopping for your trousseau. Hint that there's going to be something *very* exciting waiting for him on his wedding night—that should keep him satisfied, shouldn't it?' His eyes nar-rowed. 'Though perhaps not. Perhaps he's as frus-trated as hell too.' He gave a cruel smile. 'You certainly kissed me as though *you* were.'

Scarlett flinched. 'Keep your sordid little accusations to yourself! You are a savage, Liam—nothing but a savage. You always have been and you always will be!'

'And you just hate it—my *savagery*—don't you? As demonstrated in your response to my kiss,' he jeered softly, shaking his head just a little in sardonic reprimand. 'But enough of your physical preferences. Have you made your mind up about my—proposition?'

Scarlett regarded him with narrowed eyes. 'Kidnap and blackmail, you mean?'

'Such a *vivid* imagination,' he countered.

She glowered at him. 'Let me get this clear,' she said slowly, trying very hard to put his back up so much that he'd change his mind about taking her. 'If I agree to act as your hostess in Australia—basically that is to come and watch over you, show you how to eat an artichoke and how to properly use a napkin—'

But to her astonishment he gave a soft, low laugh. 'It's licking my knife that I can't seem to stop doing—that's what I really need help with.'

She stared at him. He was teasing her. And somehow that hurt and confused her. Their relationship had been nothing but fire and passion; there had been few laughs or light-hearted moments as they'd struggled to make a go of their ill-starred marriage. Laughter, she realised with a pang, could be very intimate, too... Momentarily she felt completely out of her depth. Could she bear to stay in the same house as him? Even for a minute?

'And how long do you anticipate I'll be staying?' she asked, realising as she asked the question that she had sealed her fate. 'How long is this house party of yours?'

'I'll need you for no more than a week,' he said, his face a devastatingly cold mask from behind which blue eyes glittered ominously.

'And if I agree,' she continued, 'then you let my stepfather off the hook?'

He shook his head. 'I'm not supplying him with any special favours,' he said. 'But I would be prepared to give him time to settle his affairs.'

And then Liam would be gone. Wouldn't he? 'And after that you'd promise to leave us all alone?' she persisted.

He gave a slow smile which was full of sexual promise. 'I honestly can't say. Because by that time you, at least, my dear Scarlett, may not want me to,' came the crushing reply.

CHAPTER FOUR

'So WHAT'S it to be?' Liam enquired silkily. 'Yes, or no?'

'But why me?' Scarlett queried in genuine astonishment. 'There must be any number of women who could play hostess for you.' They were probably three-deep, queueing round the block!

'Sure there are,' he agreed. 'But it isn't them I want, Scarlett—it's you.'

'But why me?' she asked again, not certain whether she would like hearing his answer.

She was right; she didn't.

'Oh, come on,' he chided. 'Use your imagination, Scarlett. Even you, surely, can appreciate the exquisite irony of it. *You*, gracing *my* table. Or doesn't that appeal to you? Perhaps you preferred me as the lowly labourer—easier for you to manipulate, wouldn't you say?'

Had she manipulated him? Maybe with hindsight she had—but at the time... It had been as though she'd had no conscious control over her behaviour—as though she'd been driven by some all-consuming force which had not responded to logic. At the time she had called it love. Now she was not so sure.

She cleared her throat, and clasped her hands together in subconscious appeal. 'If I agree, then

I need your word that you'll disappear from my life. That's far more important to me than saving Humphrey's skin.'

'And why's that?' he queried softly.

'You know why.'

He gave a cynical smile. 'I know that I can't seem to keep my hands off you.'

'Exactly.'

'And the feeling seems to be entirely mutual,' he observed. 'I can't see Henry being very happy about that happening after the wedding.'

'You have absolutely *no* morals,' she said, appalled by his frankness, and even more appalled by the truth in what he said.

He shrugged, then said in that deep, drawling voice, 'Call me names if it makes you feel better— it's called sublimation, Scarlett.'

With a razor-sharp tongue like that he should have been a lawyer, she thought bitterly.

'So will you do it?' he queried softly.

'It seems that I have no choice.'

His eyes glittered. 'How well I know the feeling,' he murmured sardonically, but surprisingly he took most of the tension out of the remark by giving a half-smile. 'Now,' he said, 'I suggest we get a few hours' sleep. We've a long day ahead of us tomorrow—'

'Sleep?' she questioned frostily. 'I don't know where you had in mind, but I'm not sleeping here.'

'Oh, come on, Scarlett.' The blue eyes moved expressively in the direction of a door off the small sitting-room. 'It's warm. It's cosy. There's a big bed next door just waiting—'

'I am *not* sleeping here, Liam—and that's an end to it.'

'I could always have the sofa . . .' But the glint in his eyes told her exactly what he was thinking— that the sofa would be only the most temporary of refuges for him. She had so nearly succumbed to him that he probably imagined she would need only the slightest encouragement to allow him access into her bed.

How could he be so insensitive? thought Scarlett furiously. Didn't he realise that it would be un- bearably painful for her to spend a night here under the circumstances? Here, where they'd first made love. How could she possibly even close her eyes, remembering all that had happened between them? And, worse still, if they stayed wouldn't she be tempted to open her arms to him in the small, dark hours, when the world could be so cold and so lonely? If he came to her could she honestly refuse him? And, knowing Liam, he would certainly try.

'I'm not staying here,' she said firmly. 'And that's that.'

He sighed, rubbed his thumb over the dark stubble of his chin, and then yawned hugely and gave a sensuous stretch, like a huge and very lethal jungle cat. 'OK.' He shrugged. 'It makes no dif- ference to me. We'll drive back to London. We'll need to get your visa there in the morning, anyway. Where's your passport?'

'In London. In my flat.' Was she *really* being this passive?

'Perfect. Let's get going, then. We'll stay there—we'll need to be up with the larks.'

'Wrong!' She gave him a chilly smile. '*I* will be staying there. You will be staying at a hotel. Or on a park bench—I couldn't really care.'

'Oh, Scarlett,' he chided. 'How could you kick your poor husband out onto the street—after the vows we once made to one another?'

Scarlett stilled. 'Just one thing, Liam. Don't ever—*ever* make fun of those vows again. Understand? They may have meant nothing to you—'

His mood changed instantly, his voice sounding as cold and as hard as a hammer striking on stone. 'Why should they have done? They were made under false pretences, weren't they, Scarlett? For didn't you lie to get me to marry you? To you, I was one more thing to possess—just like a favourite pony, your first car. You wanted me. And you were prepared to do anything to get me, weren't you? Even lie...'

Scarlett recoiled from the naked aggression which momentarily distorted Liam's features, seeing really and truly for the first time just how much he loathed her. And how did she feel about him? It was painfully simple. Try as she might she couldn't hate him back—he was too deeply enmeshed in her heart for that. And as long as Liam was around he would represent an overwhelming temptation which she found almost impossible to fight.

She raised her golden eyes, to be caught in the blue fire which flared from his.

'Ready to go?' he asked in a clipped tone, and she nodded mutely, wondering if he really would be true to his word and leave them all alone after she'd done this one bizarre 'favour' for him. Yet, knowing in her heart of hearts that she *wanted* to help him, she was curious to know something of his life now. And didn't she owe him one? For hadn't she messed up his life all those years ago— far more, really, than he'd ever messed up hers?

'Here. Wear this.' And he held open a black cashmere overcoat for her to put on. It was soft and deliciously warm, like being enveloped in a snug cocoon. It was obviously his coat, since it carried his own distinctively indefinable yet very masculine scent. On Liam it probably came to just below the knee, while on Scarlett it brushed the snowy ground as she preceded him out of the cottage.

'There are some gloves in the pocket,' he told her, and she found them and slipped her tiny hands inside the soft leather which swamped them.

With the moon transforming the dazzling snow into a wonderland, Scarlett felt just like the child in her favourite story, who had gone through the wardrobe door and found herself in a strange new world.

She would have to be very wary—for hadn't that always been part of Liam's own particular charm? That he had the ability to transform the normal into the wonderful and extraordinary? And that was not why she was travelling with him all the way to his home in Australia. He was forcing her to do something for him because in some primitive way he wanted to pay her back for everything that had happened all those years ago. For him, this revenge was no doubt exceptionally sweet. That she still found him the most attractive man on earth was nothing but an added complication.

That he, too, found her equally attractive obviously did not worry him in the slightest. But then, he would probably be quite happy to briefly resurrect their physical relationship and then walk away from it. She would not, she knew, be able to do likewise.

As he started to drive the snow began to fall again, until soon it was a thick, swirling flurry which even the efficient windscreen wipers had difficulty in disposing of.

'Damn!' he swore softly, as he peered ahead with narrowed eyes. 'I knew that we shouldn't have attempted to drive tonight. If we break down, Scarlett, I shall have to take you to task...'

'You seem to make a habit out of always blaming me,' she responded tartly, more to distract herself than anything else, because when he spoke in that low, slumberous tone it sounded less like an admonishment and more like an irresistible challenge. 'Don't you ever hold yourself responsible for your own actions?'

He shot her a swift look before turning away, his profile unreadable. 'Oh, for sure,' he said, in an odd kind of voice, and Scarlett wondered to just what he had been referring. But then his attention was all taken up by trying to keep the car on the increasingly icy road, and he didn't elaborate further.

The journey was a nightmare, and at one point the Porsche veered off the road very slightly. Scarlett found herself thrown forward, but was saved from hitting the windscreen by the seatbelt. Liam promptly switched off the engine and caught her by the shoulders, his fingers biting into her, his eyes raking over her. 'Are you hurt?' he demanded.

'Just shaken. Is—everything all right?'

'Sure,' he said grimly. 'We're stuck in a snow-drift on what is probably the worst night this century—we couldn't be better.'

She ignored the sarcasm. 'So what are we going to do?'

He threw her a dark look. 'Folklore has it that huddling together for warmth is the best antidote to freezing to death, but I think things might get a little out of hand if *we* happened to try it.'

'Speak for yourself!' she retorted.

'Oh, I do. I do.' He swore softly beneath his breath as he opened the door and levered his long legs out of the car. 'There's a spade in the back— I'll try and dig the wheels free.'

'I'll help you—'

'*You* will stay put.'

'But I want—'

'I don't give a *damn* what *you* want, Scarlett!' he exploded. 'It's because of you that we're here and we're stuck. Now, either you sit tight and shut up, or I'll be forced to put you over my knee. On

second thoughts—' and here, surprisingly and dis-
armingly, he grinned at her sagely '—that too might
get out of hand. Do me a favour, Scarlett, and just
stay inside and keep warm.'

So she was forced to sit and watch as he applied
that spectacular strength to removing the drifts of
snow which imprisoned them, and Scarlett was reminded all too vividly of the times when she had
watched him, clad only in his jeans, while he
wielded a similar shovel. Only tonight he was more
incongruously dressed, in that immaculately cut
dinner jacket and trousers. He must be *freezing*,
she thought anxiously.

She opened the car door, and a gust of icy wind
nearly knocked her onto the ground.

'Liam!' she called.

'Shut the bloody door!' he responded through
gritted teeth, the movement of his spade not fal-
tering for a second.

'But you'll catch your death! Do you want this
coat?'

'In a minute. Now get back in the car!'

She obeyed, cursing him silently under her breath
for that cavalier way he had of ordering her about.
She waited until he had finished, had put the spade
away and climbed wearily back into the car. She
took one look at him and began pulling off the
cashmere coat.

'I don't want to hear a word of argument from
you, Liam Rouse. You're to put this coat on. *Now*!'
But then she noticed that his suit was absolutely
cold and wet through. 'You'll have to strip off first,'

she said coolly, and he gave her a hooded look. 'Unless you *want* to catch pneumonia! Don't worry—I won't look,' she added sarcastically.

'I perform better in front of an audience,' he managed to drawl as he shrugged out of the sodden jacket, and Scarlett closed her eyes rapidly, not so much to hide the sight of the magnificent body which was about to be revealed, but to conceal from him the flashing spear of jealousy in her eyes, brought on by his provocative remark about audiences.

And oh, how it hurt. She knew that it shouldn't—but, *oh*, if she could get her hands on any woman whom Liam had stripped off in front of...

But that's crazy, she thought. You're almost divorced. You haven't seen each other in ten years. Why *shouldn't* he have slept with other women? Just because *she* hadn't had another man near her in all that time. Her stomach knotted and she gave a small, uncontrollable shiver as she heard the rasping sound of a zip being undone.

'Getting excited, Scarlett?' came the deep, mocking taunt. 'Want to help me take them off?'

Damn him for noticing! She pretended to yawn. 'Get a move on!' she told him. 'It's terribly boring just sitting here!' She could feel him wriggling out of his trousers beside her.

'Want to think of something to do to pass the time?'

'Yes, get the bloody car started and get me home!'

And at her words the engine roared into power. She opened her eyes in astonishment, to see that he had removed his clothes and was sitting clad in the black cashmere coat. As he pushed his foot down on the accelerator a bare, brown and very muscular thigh shot forward, and—thank heavens—she caught a glimpse of a pair of black boxer shorts. So he wasn't *completely* naked underneath!

'If you could manage to tear your eyes away for just a minute,' he drawled sardonically, 'you could try looking out of the window and warning me about any hazards I'm about to encounter.'

'Sure,' she said tightly, not wanting to do that at all, wishing that she could simply close her eyes and go to sleep, blot out the unwelcome and over-whelming awareness that Liam, her Liam—no, she corrected herself firmly, most definitely not *her* Liam—was sitting inches away from her wearing very little indeed.

And the most infuriating thing was that he should have looked ridiculous, dressed the way he was. But he didn't. He looked absolutely gorgeous—so much so that she was certain that if any leading fashion-house designers had seen Liam dressed in shoes and socks, boxer shorts and cashmere coat they would have marketed the look instantly!

The roads were much lighter once they hit the outskirts of London—most of the snow had already melted, and lorries were already out scattering salt.

'Wake up!' A deep voice wandered into her subconscious.

'What?' Scarlett blinked to find that she *had* actually been nodding off. He had turned the heater up full blast and was playing some lovely music that she didn't recognise, and consequently the car had become like a warm and cosy little nest, lulling her off to sleep.

She glanced at her watch. It was almost three o'clock in the morning. She eyed the familiar streets of Earls Court with a growing suspicion which grew into a horrible certainty as he confidently directed the powerful car through the maze of streets. 'You know where I live!' she accused him.

'That's right,' he agreed as he drew up outside the large grey house where she had the basement flat.

But how? she wondered in confusion. And more importantly—*why*? 'How come?' she asked bluntly.

He switched off the engine and turned towards her. 'Mmm?'

'How do you know where I live?' she repeated impatiently.

With the faint orange nimbus of the streetlamp casting strange and almost satanic lights over the sculpted features of his face, it was impossible to gauge what he was thinking.

He shrugged. 'I've always maintained a certain...interest, shall we say?...in how you'd turned out.'

Her heart began pattering. 'You mean, you've been having me watched for all these years?'

He gave a low laugh. 'Oh, that imagination of yours, Scarlett—you really must try to curb it! No, nothing quite so dramatic as that. I didn't really need to. After the split you managed to give yourself a pretty high profile. I read about your exploits in the newspapers—you seemed hell-bent on partying yourself to death.'

As she heard the grating disapproval in his voice she silently thanked the streetlights for their protective half-light. Yes, she'd gone on an endless round of partying and clubbing late into the night. Every society event, every first night, every art gallery opening—Scarlett had been there. As if by filling every waking moment she might bring to life again the part of her that had died when Liam had left her.

But it hadn't worked. The frenetic social round had done nothing other than convince her that they were nothing more than shallow, worthless events, full of shallow, worthless people. In fact, they had served to emphasise the gulf between those kinds of people and the man she had married.

He was very still as he studied her, his kissable mouth curved into a sardonic slash. 'So I did you a favour, did I, Scarlett? By leaving I gave you the opportunity to play the field with all those eminently *eligible* candidates. I'll bet Humphrey was delighted.'

Scarlett drew her chin up. Yes, Humphrey *had* been delighted. But as for playing the field—huh!— the very thought was laughable. It had been years before she could even bring herself to let a man touch her, and no man had ever touched her in the way that Liam had—body *or* soul. When Liam had gone she'd felt as though a little part of her had shrivelled up and died, never to be resurrected again.

Her gold eyes glittered. But let Liam continue to live in his pathetic little stereotypical world. If he wanted to think of her as the feckless society bimbo—then damn well let him!

'Yes, it was enormous fun!' she lied brightly, before the fatigue returned to wash over her again. She let her eyelids slip down over her eyes, then stifled a yawn.

'Let's get inside.' His voice sounded suddenly urgent, with an underlying huskiness, and she knew exactly what *that* meant. Surely he hadn't found a mere yawn provocative? But there again, knowing Liam, he probably had.

'You're not coming inside,' she said, far too quickly. 'Where are you staying?'

He gave a lazy smile. 'Oh, Scarlett—you're not planning to make me walk into the Ritz wearing this?' He shifted one leg slightly, and she was confronted by that naked thigh all over again. 'I'll be arrested for indecent exposure. Not to mention your alleged kidnap!'

'It would serve you right!' she snapped. But he was laughing, and the look in his blue eyes was irresistible—and perhaps she was still in some kind of shock, because she could hardly stop laughing herself as she pictured him walking into one of London's top hotels wearing a pair of black boxer shorts and a cashmere coat! 'Oh, all right,' she said crossly. 'You'd better come inside!'

She tried to justify it as they made their way down the steps. You couldn't just turn someone out into the cold on a horrible night like this. Not when they'd just dug you out of a snow-filled ditch. Especially someone you'd once been married to. Someone you'd once cared a very great deal for.

And then a dreadful thought occurred to her. 'I don't have a key!' she exclaimed, remembering how he'd hijacked her from the party.

'You don't keep one under a brick by the front door?'

She gave him a withering look. 'This is *London*, Liam, not Toytown!'

'Then I guess it's both of us back to the Ritz, impending arrest or not.'

No way! If he thought she was going to sample the luxury of one of London's best hotels with him, he had another think coming. 'The girl in the flat upstairs has a key,' she said reluctantly. 'Though she'll kill me for waking her at this hour.'

But Michelle didn't kill her; she was still up. Instead her eyes nearly popped out of her head when she opened the door to see Scarlett in all her evening finery with the peculiarly dressed Liam beside her.

'I hadn't gone to bed; I've got a few friends who're still here,' she explained, her gaze flicking appraisingly over Liam. 'I thought you were away for the weekend, getting engaged?' She smiled at Liam with the look of a tiger cub let loose in a butcher's shop. 'Tell you what—why don't you both come in for a drink? You look as though you could

use one.' She smiled at Liam again. 'Or just leave
your friend, Scarlett, if you want to get to bed...'

Did Liam deliberately choose that moment,
Scarlett wondered, to lean against the doorjamb so
that the black coat gaped to reveal exactly what he
had on underneath? Or rather, what he *didn't* have
on underneath, more to the point. And those boxer
shorts were more suited to the kind of male stripper
who had women at hen nights falling at their feet!
she thought furiously. Or maybe it was just the way
he wore them...

'Just the key, please, Michelle,' he said lazily.
'You see, we're *both* very tired, and we can't wait
to get into bed—can we, Scarlett?'

Scarlett waited until they were safely inside her
flat, with the door closed behind them, before she
let rip. 'How *dare* you?' she exploded.

'What's the matter?' he enquired, going straight
to the central heating thermostat and turning it up
high—as if he *owned* the place.

'Don't play the innocent with me! You knew
exactly what you were doing! Letting Michelle think
that we were going to—going to—'

'Going to what?' he enquired helpfully.

She stared at him in horror. 'What if she tells
Henry?'

The blue eyes were suddenly frighteningly and
icily cold. 'Not my problem,' he said dismissively,
his mouth twisting derisively at the mention of her
fiancé's name.

She glared at him as he wandered over towards one of the doors leading off the sitting-room. 'That's *my* bedroom,' she said pointedly.

'And this one?'

Oh, heavens—she didn't want him snooping around her study. The less he learnt about her life, the less involvement he had in it—and the easier it would be to forget him again. 'That's a junk room,' she said dismissively. 'You can have the sofa.' Then, in order to distract him from his guided tour, she said, 'I'm making myself a hot drink. Do you want one?'

'Please.' And he walked over to the sofa and sank down on it.

She made them hot whisky toddies, which tasted wonderful. She stole a glance at him as she put her glass down. He was now lying sprawled all over her sofa, still in that ridiculous outfit, looking, she thought with a sudden pang, as though he belonged there. The whole thing was crazy—bizarre. Maybe when she woke up in the morning she would find it had all been one long, bad dream, and he would be gone.

Scarlett went to the linen cupboard in the hall, took out some bedding and threw it down on top of him. 'There! I'm going to bed! And don't think you can try any of your tricks, Liam.'

His eyes glinted. 'Tricks?'

'I shall be locking the door,' she said pointedly.

'You don't think that a locked door would keep me out, do you, Scarlett?' he enquired softly.

'I suppose you mean that you'd smash it down,' she said. 'That's more your style, isn't it?' And then she wished she hadn't as she saw his face darken. He was remembering that last terrible row, she thought, when he'd put his fist through the panel of the door.

'I mean that you'd probably wake up in the middle of the night, remember that I'm here and unlock it yourself,' he replied arrogantly as he kicked off his shoes.

She stood there watching him, furiously searching for a sharp retort. Then she saw that the coat was about to be discarded, and, deciding that verbal supremacy was irrelevant when confronted with the sight of a near-naked Liam, Scarlett fled.

CHAPTER FIVE

BUT Scarlett couldn't sleep. Had she ever really expected to? Knowing...knowing that Liam lay mere feet away from her, making it impossible not to yearn to be in his arms again. But though the yearnings were torment enough, they were nothing when compared to the memories which refused to go away. Powerful, poignant memories, which swept over her like an unremitting sea. And the long years seemed to vanish as they mocked her...

All those years ago.

The economic climate had been very different then. Scarlett's mother had remarried just a year after Scarlett's father's death and Scarlett could not have failed to be aware of her new stepfather's lavish wealth. Materially, at least, she had been immensely privileged.

She had gone to the best schools, she had ridden the best horses, her friends had been the daughters of other, equally rich men. But her brother had been away at school, and the newly married couple had excluded her almost completely. Scarlett had been desperately lonely.

Then, when she was ten, Liam had arrived, and her life had changed forever.

His widowed mother came to work on her step-father's estate, bringing with her the twelve-year-old Liam.

Scarlett could remember seeing him for the first time as vividly as if it had happened last week. At twelve he was already tall and dark, with all the promise of the superb body he would develop throughout his teens. He was so unlike the other boys she knew—the ones with their clipped public school accents and their ideas of life already formed for them by their parents.

Even at twelve, Liam viewed life with a cynicism way beyond his years as he acknowledged the inequalities of the world. He went to the small local school, and he always seemed to have his head in a book. He excelled at everything he turned his hand to—those cold, clever eyes absorbing everything. And even at that age there was something about him that set him apart from the others.

Instinctively a loner, he nevertheless had a soft spot for Scarlett. Perhaps he saw through to her own loneliness; maybe the early loss of his own father made him gentler with her than with the others—whatever it was, he let her tag along, and she hero-worshipped him in return.

In Scarlett's eyes, Liam could say or do no wrong. She used to listen to him wide-eyed while he talked to her passionately about the world he was going to see—every single inch of it.

'You're always reading,' she complained one day, when she was about fifteen. 'Why don't you give yourself a break once in a while?'

'Because it's my only way out,' he said simply, looking at her with eyes as blue as the great oceans he was always reading about.

'What do you mean? Way out of what?'

'The class I've been born into.' He smiled. 'Education. That's the only way out. Now shut up, Scarlett—there's a good girl—and read that Huxley I lent you.'

The summer after Liam took his A levels—getting the best grades ever recorded in his school—he took a year out and went off to 'do' Europe, before going up to university.

Scarlett missed him more than she would have thought possible. At sixteen she was just entering into the social whirl, and she found herself looking at a life which seemed to stretch yawningly ahead of her—a constant stream of balls and cocktail parties, of hunting and fashion shows. She was always meeting the type of man she would one day be expected to marry. And every one of them bored her rigid.

And then one day during the summer holidays, when Scarlett was seventeen, Liam came home from Europe.

Sir Humphrey announced at breakfast one morning that Mrs Rouse's son looked as strong as an ox, and that he had promptly employed Liam to do manual work on the estate until he went off to college in the autumn.

But nothing was the same any more. Something had changed between Liam and Scarlett.

Scarlett stared up at the boy who had become such a stunning man, and met what seemed to be his habitual flinty stare with miserable enlightenment. Gone was that easy familiarity they'd always shared. And in its place was a new and uncomfortable awareness, something which made her senses tingle with excitement, while Liam seemed not to like her very much at all any more.

He seemed to go out of his way to avoid her, barely able to bring himself to speak to her civilly.

'I hate you, Liam Rouse!' she sobbed into her pillow one night. And two could play at the game of ignoring, she thought defiantly. So she went to her tennis parties, accepted lifts home in sports cars, and forced herself to laugh uproariously whenever she spotted that dark, brooding figure. And Liam stayed immune to it all.

But one day she came across him unexpectedly in the forest—she'd been out riding on her favourite frisky black mare. Sable had cantered into a clearing and there had been Liam, stripped to the waist, felling logs.

He glanced up briefly, his eyes flicking over her dismissively, then turned back to his work, saying not a word.

Scarlett stared at him with a growing anger which quickly became a frightening kind of awareness. He was stripped to the waist, wearing nothing but a pair of very old jeans which clung lovingly to narrow, lean hips. Through a slashing rip over one hard thigh Scarlett could see solid muscle. But it was the play of muscles over his bare back which fascinated her most—endless patterns of perfect strength. She watched as he effortlessly lifted the axe in a sweeping movement, saw the sweat running down to be soaked up by the waistband of those indecently fitting jeans.

And all of a sudden she'd had enough! How dared he ignore her—treat her as though she was invisible? Temper snapping, she slapped her riding crop against her jodhpured thigh. 'What's got into you all of a sudden, Liam Rouse?' she demanded, tossing her hair back over her shoulders. 'Why are you being so horrible to me?'

The dark head was raised as he leaned on his axe, and the eyes lifted silently to her face, flicking down to the agitated rise and fall of her breasts as they heaved against the scarlet T-shirt she wore.

He shook his head. 'Go away, Scarlett,' he said wearily, and picked up his axe as if to resume chopping.

'I won't go away!' she returned spiritedly. 'At least—not until you tell me why it is you don't act like my friend any more.'

'Maybe it's because that seems the most sensible solution for everyone concerned,' he said coolly.

She still didn't understand. 'But we were *friends*, Liam—once!' she pleaded. 'Friends!'

'And things change,' he said abruptly as he turned his back.

It was nothing but the most blatant and unforgivable rudeness, and with a snort of anger Scarlett turned the horse and cantered off without another word, vowing never to waste her time speaking to him again.

But some demon inside her drove her to do just what she'd sworn not to, and the very next day she was back.

Again he looked up at her briefly, his eyes narrowing as he took in her slender jodhpured figure astride the horse, the faintly diaphanous white silk of her shirt blowing gently in the breeze. He picked up his axe and started smashing it against a log.

Oh, why couldn't it be like it used to be? she thought yearningly. She began fishing around in her saddlebag. 'Would you like a drink?' she called out to him.

He stared at her, a deep searching stare, as she raised the bottle to her lips and drank some ice-cold cola, before holding it out to him. 'Here,' she said.

He hesitated before moving forward and accepting the bottle, drinking from it thirstily, and Scarlett felt as triumphant as if she'd just broken a beautiful but spirited new horse.

'Thanks,' he said, and licked a drop of cola from his upper lip.

Scarlett was mesmerised by the movement. Her heart began to pound explosively and her cheeks flared with an uncomfortable fire; she knew that those blue eyes would notice her discomfiture.

They did. And something about him seemed to change. The muscular frame relaxed, and he gave a slow, lazy smile showing brilliant white teeth. The arrogant smile of a man who knew damn well what she had just been thinking. Angrily Scarlett picked up her reins.

'Going already?' he queried.

'I can't think why!' she retorted. 'When I receive such an overwhelming welcome!'

He laughed, then, sounding much more like the old Liam.

'You coming this way tomorrow?' he queried.

'I doubt it,' she told him frostily, sticking her small snub nose in the air, and she heard the sound of his mocking laughter as she took the horse full-stretch into a gallop.

But she did go back the next day. And the next. And to her delight she found they still had an awful lot to talk about. She started taking him lunch, just like in the old days—except that in the old days Scarlett couldn't remember lovingly observing every detail of him, the way she seemed to these days.

She loved watching him eat, loved watching him chop logs. She loved watching him do absolutely *anything*. She longed with an aching yearning for him to kiss her, but he didn't, even though—*surely*—he could feel the tension which buzzed in the air between them, like an electric cable gone out of control.

Instead, he described his dreams and his plans, just as he'd always done, and she tried very hard to be interested when all she wanted was to feel his arms around her.

'I've decided to read PPE at university,' he told her one day, having hurled a decimated apple core into the undergrowth. He leaned back against the sturdy trunk of the oak tree and shut his eyes. 'First I'm going to make a pile of money, and then I'm going to change the world.'

'How?' asked Scarlett, laughing as she rolled a leaf between her fingertips, then flicked it to see how far it would go.

He shrugged. 'Who knows? But I'll find a way.' The sapphire-blue eyes snapped open. 'And what about you, Scarlett? What are you planning to do with your life?'

I want to spend it with you, she thought suddenly, lifting her narrow shoulders upwards as she searched around for something conventional. 'I don't know, really. I haven't given it a lot of thought.'

God, she had been so mediocre, so unambitious. It made her cringe now when she thought back to the person she'd been then.

'Well, you should think about it—you've got your whole life ahead of you. Why don't you take up art? You know how good you are.'

'I'm not *that* good,' she said stubbornly.

'Sure you are! You ought to go away to art college.'

But the thought of going away for three years, of not seeing Liam at every available opportunity, filled her with horror. 'Oh, I can't be doing with all that,' she said quickly, seeing his disapproving look as she voiced her lack of ambition.

'But what will you do?' he persisted.

Scarlett shrugged. 'Oh, fill in, I guess. Until I get married.' To you. The words seemed to hang on the air as though she'd actually said them.

As soon as she'd said it, she regretted it. It was terribly *infra dig* to admit to wanting to settle down—particularly at the tender age of seventeen.

Liam shifted his position from the tree and stood up abruptly. 'You'd better go,' he said, almost harshly, and the forbidding stranger had taken his place again. 'I've got work to do.'

'OK.' She stood up, and the thick black silky ponytail of hair streamed down her back. 'I'll see you tomorrow—'

'*No.*' His voice was decisive; all the friendliness had fled from his face. 'Not tomorrow, Scarlett. Not any day—do you understand? It's not a good idea—we can't keep seeing one another!'

Her face went pale and her mouth trembled. Who the hell did he think he was? She ran over to Sable and swung herself up onto the horse's back without another word, but he followed her, and caught her foot in his hand. It looked a very tiny foot in such a big, callused hand.

'Do you understand what I'm saying to you, Scarlett?' he said urgently. 'It isn't the same between us any more! It *can't* be! Don't you understand that?'

No, she didn't, but she was damned if she'd admit it. She gave him a superior smile. 'What a *dreadful* fuss you make over nothing, Liam—'

To her astonishment he swung himself up to join her on the horse's back with a light and natural grace which didn't even cause the slightest whinny of protest from the horse. He caught hold of Scarlett's shoulders and turned her round, his eyes burning as they stared down into her face.

He kissed her.

He kissed her like a man crazy for her.

It frightened her, and it thrilled her like mad. She wanted it to go on forever, and for a little while it seemed as if it did, and she felt as though she'd taken a one-way ticket to heaven. He stopped only because she was gasping for breath, and when she dazedly stared at him she saw that his eyes looked back and his face was filled with...what? Fury, yes, but something else too—regret?

'Now do you understand, Scarlett?' he ground out. 'Do you?'

'I—I think so,' she stammered.

He jumped off the horse, picked the reins up and handed them to her. 'Then stay away from me!' he warned, and slapped Sable's rump so that she trotted away, carrying her dazed mistress with her.

She stayed away from the forest and tried to put Liam out of her mind, but it was impossible. She was completely obsessed by him.

Then she started hearing whispers in the village. That Liam had been seen out with one of the local girls—a scrumptious blonde named Jenna, who had the classic peaches-and-cream beauty. And Scarlett knew her first taste of deep, black jealousy.

With a renewed fervour she threw herself into the dizzying round of summer parties organised at the grand houses in the county, but nothing seemed to work. It was Liam whose face haunted her dreams, the memories of Liam's kiss which set her heart pounding.

Her rides grew longer. She galloped recklessly over fields, trotted out along the country lanes—but all to no avail. She felt as tense as a coiled-up spring.

One day she rode further than ever before, towards an old derelict cottage on the outskirts of the estate, and within half a mile she sensed his presence; it was as tangible as that. Or perhaps subconsciously she had heard that Liam was working on this section of the land—perhaps this was where he brought Jenna sometimes...

She saw him straight away. He was standing at the top of a ladder, hammering something onto the roof. As she approached he looked over his shoulder and down at her.

And stayed looking.

She knew that she looked wild. She was hatless and her raven-black hair spilled in wild disarray over her shoulders, contrasting with the snowy white of her silk riding shirt.

They stayed like that, just staring for long moments. 'Hello, Scarlett,' he said eventually.

She had expected more of his rage, more of his orders to keep away, and to hear his gorgeous deep voice back to normal completely disarmed her. It was so stupid not to be speaking when she liked him more than anyone else in the world. 'Hello, Liam,' she said, giving him a wide smile as she dismounted and tied Sable to a tree.

He was climbing down the ladder, looking more at home in his own skin than anyone else she'd ever seen. He moved with all the stealth and grace of some thoroughbred stallion, she thought with slightly unwilling admiration, and she found herself covertly watching the powerful thrust of his thighs. He turned to face her at the bottom and gave her a slow, almost sad smile. The blue of his denim shirt was the same intense blue as his eyes.

'Are you thirsty?' she offered hopefully.

He shook his head. 'No.'

And something in the look on his face made her realise the foolishness of her question. 'No, I guess you're not.' She pushed a lock of black hair off her face. 'How's Jenna?' she asked casually, taking care to keep the demon jealousy from her voice.

He glowered. 'How the hell should I know?'

'I thought you were seeing her.'

'Well, you thought wrong!' he almost shouted.

She stared at him in confusion. The friendliness had flown from his face, and the tension was back with a vengeance. 'Liam, I—'

But her appeal was never made, because suddenly she was in his arms and he was kissing her mouth, her neck, her shoulders, and she was kissing him back, her untutored mouth quickly learning from his. In seconds, it seemed, he had opened the buttons of her shirt and pushed it impatiently off her shoulders. It fluttered to the forest floor, so that she was clad in nothing but her jodhpurs and a tiny lacy white brassière.

With a shudder she felt him touch her breasts, hearing him give a husky moan as he caressed each swollen mound, massaging each hardened tip between finger and thumb through the thin material of the bra, and she, thrilled beyond belief, found herself watching the movement of his hands, so very dark against the white fabric. And when he unclipped the bra, and she was naked to the waist, it was her turn to moan as he bent his dark head to tease and tug and suckle sweetly on one deliciously hard nipple, and she had to clutch his head for support.

'Oh, Liam,' she breathed softly. 'Please ...'

'I know,' he soothed, and he suckled her again.

'Please ...' she repeated, on a note of wonder. 'Please don't stop.' Don't ever stop.

'I won't,' he whispered, almost gently, as he kissed the top of her head. 'It's the same for me, you know.' And he picked her up and effortlessly carried her into the cottage.

She knew where all this was going to lead; of course she did. She was seventeen and she knew the facts of life. Perhaps she should have been scared by the look of intense hunger on the face of the man, or disturbed by just how aroused he very obviously was. But her desire for Liam went deeper than a physical ache which demanded relief—because she recognised then that she loved him, that in a way she had always loved him.

He pulled his shirt off roughly and threw it onto the bare boards, before lying her on top of it as if he were offering her a feather bed.

His hands were so sure, their movements bestowing on her undreamt-of delights. And as he took her clothes off she teetered between helpless pleasure and a growing impatience to lie naked next to him. She scrabbled at the button on his jeans, and she heard him laugh softly.

'Little wildcat!' he admonished. 'I dreamt that you'd be like this, Scarlett.'

In answer she gently scraped her nails down the broad back, and he laughed again while he hooked his fingers inside her panties and slid them down her legs. She watched, hypnotised and fascinated, as he gingerly unzipped his jeans and wriggled out of them. Scarlett's throat tightened and dried as she saw for herself the massive male power of him.

Like someone in the middle of the most delicious dream, she reached her hand out to touch him, but he reared away like an angry stallion, taking both her hands and pinning them above her head, until she submitted completely to the demands of his mouth as it awakened nebulous hungers in her which demanded to be assuaged.

Things got rapidly out of control. Once, just before he took her, he tried to move away, his hand groping blindly for the pocket of his jeans, but Scarlett was urged on by some instinct which seemed to flare up from deep within her. She wanted to feel *him*—just him—inside her. Liam without any barrier coming between them on this first union. And she found herself imprisoning him with her naked legs, inciting him with frantic little circlings of her hips.

She heard him give a long, low moan as he thrust into her once, then again and again—deeper and deeper. And then it was like hurtling at breakneck speed down a precipitous mountain. She felt the incredible tension in both of them reach an unbearable pitch.

'Oh, my God, Scarlett,' she remembered him saying, in a tortured kind of voice.

She thought she was going to die with the sweet pleasure of it. 'Oh, Liam,' she whispered, her voice breaking with the sheer emotion of wanting to tell him the most important thing in the world. 'I love you!'

Their eyes met for that timeless instant before they were completely engulfed, and Scarlett fell sobbing into his arms . . .

Scarlett sat bolt upright in bed and buried her head in her hands, wanting to cry out her distress into the unwelcoming night but not daring to, lest she waken Liam next door.

Restlessly she got up from the bed and quietly left the room to fetch herself a drink of water, but as she padded silently across the sitting-room it was unfortunate that her eyes strayed to the sofa, to find her estranged husband lying on his side, his head cradled on one arm, sleeping like a baby. And the wretched duvet had slipped to the floor, leaving him exposed and as beautifully naked as the day he had been born.

The thought brought with it a desperate moment of sadness for his mother. How disappointed she must have been at their shotgun wedding, to have watched her dreams of seeing her only son going off to university smashed to the ground. Scarlett felt suddenly ashamed, aware that she had been so wrapped up in her own problems at the time that she hadn't really given it a thought.

She watched him stir a little, saw him rub that broad brown shoulder in his sleep. She told herself that anyone with any kind of heart would have crept over and picked the duvet up and carefully covered his sleeping form with it. He'd already had one freezing that day, and, though she might hate him, she didn't hate him enough to want to see him sick.

But what was it that made her pause for a second longer as she tucked it gently around his shoulders? Remembering the nights that those strong arms had enfolded her in the blissfully heady early days of their ill-fated relationship...?

After that first rapturous lovemaking they had carried on meeting clandestinely at the cottage, but their snatched moments and their long lunches together had lost their innocence. Scarlett had discovered love and she had discovered sex, and she hadn't been able to get enough of either. The cottage, and the grounds that surrounded it, had become their private and erotic haven.

One day, they lay naked and entwined on a bed of tiny twigs and moss and bracken, Scarlett's body shaking as she coasted into heaven. 'Oh. *Oh*. Oh, *Liam,*' she breathed, sensing his own imminent release as he shuddered against her.

'No,' she murmured languorously as she felt him begin to pull away from her. 'Don't move an inch.' She wrapped her arms around his back. 'Stay exactly like that.'

He gave a long, low laugh against her neck. 'But, sweetheart. If I do that, then you know what's going to happen all over again?'

She wriggled her bare breasts against his hair-roughened chest, and felt him—incredibly—swell to fill her yet again. 'No?' she whispered. 'What?'

He gave a small groan as he moved. 'This,' he said, as he thrust against her. 'God, Scarlett. I didn't think it was possible to want to make love like this all day.'

And never stop, she thought rapturously as she gave herself up to the soaring pleasure.

'I love you,' she whispered afterwards.

But, as usual, there was silence.

'Liam?'

He lifted her hand to his mouth and kissed it. 'You only *think* you love me,' he said. 'You've just discovered sex, that's all.'

She tried to wriggle out from beneath him, but he wouldn't let her. 'You're just spoiling everything,' she protested. 'You make it sound so—*ordinary.*'

'It isn't ordinary,' he contradicted gently. 'It's beautiful, special. But—'

That sounded like love to *her*. 'But—what?'

'Sweetheart, we're both so young,' he said gently. 'You're barely eighteen, and I'm due to go off to college for three years next month. We can't look into the future, predict what's going to happen. So let's take things one day at a time, hmm?'

Even though she knew he spoke sense, his words were the death knell to her dreams. She often wondered what would have happened if she hadn't missed her period.

She waited before she told him, sure that she must be mistaken, but so edgy with fear that she was sure he would notice.

He did. One afternoon his blue eyes narrowed as he bent his head to look down into her pale face. 'Something's wrong,' he stated. 'What is it, Scarlett?'

She had rehearsed all kinds of ways to say it, but in the end she just blurted it out. 'I think I'm pregnant.' There, now it was out. She'd expected anger, recriminations, but apart from a muscle working furiously in the side of his face he remained very calm.

'How late are you?'

She swallowed. 'Almost three weeks.'

He swore then, softly. 'Why the hell didn't you tell me sooner?'

Because she had been afraid of his reaction—terrified that he would just disappear from her life leaving her to face it all on her own. Because what man wanted to be saddled with a baby when he was twenty years old and on the brink of his life?

'Because I wanted to be sure.'

'And how sure are you?'

She closed her eyes briefly, then opened them again. 'Almost positive.' She shook her head. 'No.

Positive. I'm never late. Ever. My—' She stumbled, embarrassed—but why on earth should she be embarrassed after all the intimacies they had shared these past weeks? 'My breasts have been very swollen and—tender.' It was a measure of how grave the situation was that he did not immediately reach out to touch them—indeed, he had not touched her once since she had told him. 'And I've been feeling sick in the mornings,' she finished baldly. 'Every morning.'

'I see.' He nodded, then turned his back on her, to gaze out at the slender brown columns of the trees which surrounded them. 'The first time we made love—I didn't use anything.'

But he had tried to, she thought guiltily. She remembered him trying to reach for his jeans. And she had stopped him.

'*Damn*!' he exploded, and he smashed his fist against the trunk of a nearby tree. 'One time. Like all the books tell you. Just the one time—that's all you need.' He turned round then, and must have seen the look of panic on her face, for his own features softened, and he leaned forward to kiss her lips with a new tenderness which in its way was just as thrilling to Scarlett as the desire which was never far from the surface. 'Will you take a test?' he quizzed gently.

Scarlett shrugged her shoulders distractedly. 'I could do—but that means either testing at the doctor's or buying a kit from the chemist. Everyone in the village will know—' She broke off and ran her hand through her tumbled black hair, but he caught it and held it close to his heart.

'Then I guess we'll just have to fix this between us,' he said quietly.

'*Fix* it?' she echoed, on a strangled whisper. 'What do you mean?'

He read the fear in her eyes and shook his head from side to side. 'Scarlett, sweetheart, there's only one possible way to fix this—and that's for us to get married. That's what you want, isn't it?'

'Oh, Liam!' she sobbed, on a note of heartfelt happiness. 'Yes! You know I do!'

'Then come here—and kiss me.'

But there was more than one cloud on their horizon—of course there was.

For a start they eloped, because Scarlett was certain that her stepfather would try to stop them marrying, and when they came back all hell broke loose. Scarlett's mother and her stepfather were mortified that she'd run off with the 'hired help'. Humphrey actually said that to her, and Liam overheard, and Scarlett refused to speak to Humphrey until he apologised.

And obviously, with a wife to support, Liam was forced to cancel his place at university, which upset his mother far more than Scarlett would ever have imagined. She was foolish enough to ask Liam why, one day.

'Well, she saw it as my opportunity to drag myself up and out of the cycle of hard work until you drop,' he told her drily. 'You see, Scarlett, I don't come from the kind of family where someone can always bail me out financially. I have to make it on my own.'

He was determined to do that, thought Scarlett. Stubbornly determined, at times—refusing Sir Humphrey's offer of a small cottage on the estate, preferring instead to rent the shabby little flat over the café in the village.

And each day Liam went out, but the manual work which had been perfectly satisfactory as a fill-in before college now palled when viewed as a life-long commitment. The books which once he had devoured so eagerly he now neglected. After a long, hard day all he wanted was a hot bath, a meal, and to make love to her without ever telling her the words she so needed to hear.

And then, when the unbelievable happened, she was too afraid to tell him that either—but this time he didn't notice that she was troubled. In fact, these days he seemed to notice very little at all... Until that one evening when he walked into their tiny, cramped bathroom just as she was getting the small cardboard box out of the cabinet, and he stopped still, an incredulous question in his eyes.

She froze.

'Scarlett?'

She stared back and saw the accusation in his eyes. She shivered.

'Scarlett?' It was ominously spoken.

'Yes!' she blurted out, in answer to the question. '*Yes!*'

He advanced towards her, his face the icy mask of a stranger, so cold and distant that her blood chilled. 'There's no baby?' he asked slowly, each word coming out as awkwardly as if he were speaking it for the first time.

She dug her nails into the palms of her hands without feeling it. 'No,' she whispered.

The expression in his eyes unnerved her. 'No baby?' he said again.

'No.'

'There never *was* any baby?' he shouted. 'Was there, Scarlett?'

How could she lie to him? 'No,' she said, her voice breaking into a sob.

'You bitch,' he said softly, and then, turning in a blind, violent movement, he smashed his fist into the thin plywood of the door, shattering it completely, and Scarlett began to shiver uncontrollably as he ran out of room.

She ran after him 'Liam!' she shouted. 'Liam! For God's sake—come back!'

But she heard his footsteps echoing down the uncarpeted steps, and she slumped to the floor, too heartbroken even for tears.

After that there was a curt little note from Liam, which arrived from London shortly after he'd left, suggesting that they meet to 'discuss the future'. But Scarlett was unable to face going, knowing what he wanted to say. She was too shocked and upset to face that derisive look on his face again, and her stepfather offered to go in her place. And when Sir Humphrey returned, one look at him told her everything she needed to know.

Liam did not want her back.

CHAPTER SIX

'WAKEY, wakey! Rise and shine!'

Scarlett half opened her eyelids, hovering on the dreamy edge of sleep and wondering what that deep and painfully familiar voice was doing in her bedroom.

Bedroom!

Her eyes snapped open and there stood Liam, with one of her handtowels wrapped around a pair of narrow hips and a tray held in his hand.

'Sleep well?' he asked roguishly.

'Yes, thank you,' she lied.

'You didn't lock the door, then?'

'There wasn't a lot of point,' she snapped. 'If you'd wanted to get in, you could have done—but don't worry, I was all prepared for you.'

'*Real-ly*?' he drawled suggestively, raising his eyebrows in appreciation.

'Yes.' She gave him a sweet smile, and lifted out the heavy statuette from underneath her pillow. 'I would have crowned you with this!'

He grinned. 'I don't believe you for a moment, Scarlett. Now, where shall I put this?' And he walked over to the bedside table, put the tray down, and sat on the edge of the bed.

'Can't you put something on?' she asked irritably. The sight of Liam wearing nothing but a hopelessly insubstantial towel which revealed those rock-hard thighs and buttocks in loving detail was playing havoc with her nerves.

'Like what? All I have is one very crumpled and still damp dinner suit. I'll have some clothes sent across from my hotel. Why?' he queried, with another positively roguish smile. 'Does it bother you—me being dressed like this?'

Undressed, more like. 'No, it doesn't!' she lied, then sighed. How had all this happened? How had he managed to infiltrate her home and her life? What on earth was she doing, with Liam sitting on the edge of her bed pouring out two cups of coffee, and her wishing that he'd push the tray aside and climb in with her?

She closed her eyes in horror. Climb in with her! Had she now gone *completely* off her rocker?

'Still take it black?' Liam raised an eyebrow in the direction of the coffee-pot, and that simple little question managed to reinforce just how well he knew her.

Had Henry ever made her coffee? she wondered suddenly. No, she didn't think he had—Henry was one of those men who always boasted that he couldn't boil an egg. When actually the implication was that they shouldn't *have* to boil an egg. That was women's work. Or servants'.

'Black?' he prompted again.

'Please.' Snap out of it, Scarlett—for pity's sake!

He proffered a plate. 'Have some toast. I could only find white bread, I'm afraid. Black mark there,

Scarlett—you should know by now that wholemeal is *much* better for you!'

It smelt delicious, but she wasn't going to give him the satisfaction of knowing that. 'I don't want any toast!' she howled. 'I want my life to be back to what it was before you came in, ruining everything!'

She paused as she took a sip of the strong coffee. After his initial display of foul temper he seemed to have calmed down a lot. Indeed, since they'd arrived at her flat he'd been almost human again. Perhaps the whole idea that she accompany him to Australia had been a cruel kind of joke. Perhaps with morning had come the light of reason, and surely if she appealed to his better nature—if he *had* one—then he might reconsider his whole hare-brained scheme.

'You seem in a very good mood this morning,' she ventured.

He smiled. 'That's because I am. A surprisingly good night's sleep—then breakfast with a beautiful woman. What more could a man ask for? *Well*—' his voice deepened to the sexiest verbal caress imaginable '—perhaps I can think of *something . . .*'

It was difficult, but she decided to ignore that. She needed to take advantage of this no doubt brief respite in his beastliness towards her.

'Liam,' she began.

'Scarlett.'

'You don't really want me to come to Australia with you, do you?'

'I do,' he said implacably. 'And if you want to save dear Sir Humphrey from financial ruin—*and* eject me from your life into the bargain—then you'll do as I ask. After all,' he murmured, 'if I stayed ... Well, Henry might get just a fraction annoyed if you continued to fall into my arms with exciting regularity. I know that *I* would, in his position.'

She put her cup down on the locker with a clatter. 'Oh, you're impossible!'

'I know,' he agreed as his cup joined hers, and before she realised what was happening he was lying on top of her, his hands on her shoulders, and he was bending his head to kiss the skin there. 'I am also,' he said, in the low, husky voice of desire which she still recognised all too well, 'very, *very* turned on by the sight of you wearing this pretty but very inadequate little thing.' And a finger moved down to follow the thin line of the satin strap of her nightdress.

'It's n-not inadequate.'

'Isn't it?' He smiled. 'Not even down here?' And he slid the duvet down to reveal her breasts.

Normally it was a perfectly decent satin night-dress, but that was because normally her breasts weren't swollen to what felt like twice their normal size, with two painfully hard tips standing proud as he gazed down at them hungrily.

'It looks pretty inadequate to me,' he said softly, and the finger moved down agonisingly slowly until it lingered on the nipple itself, and Scarlett felt a sharp pleasure stabbing there, which started to sizzle through every fibre of her body. 'Don't you think so?'

'I...' Stop him! For God's sake stop him! But now he was kissing her neck, and she closed her eyes in desperation, knowing that she couldn't stop him, not for all the tea in China.

'Is it any more decent down here?' he murmured, and then he was sliding the duvet all the way down, and she was doing absolutely nothing about it. 'Mmm?' His mouth had left her neck, was slowly moving down. 'Is it?'

Oh, my God. Now he was slipping one of the tiny shoestring straps down, and had exposed one whole and aching breast. There was not a thing she could do about it as that dark head captured one tormented nub to suckle on it, and the pleasure was so acute that Scarlett actually felt consciousness recede.

He started pushing up the white satin which lay in folds rucked around her knees to expose her creamy thighs, which were already parting in anticipation, and her eyelids flickered open to see, through the towel, that he was incredibly and hopelessly aroused.

'God, Scarlett,' he said harshly, on an almost unrecognisable note of desire. 'I *want* you. Right now.'

Her head fell back as his fingertips stroked their way up the satin skin of her inner thigh.

'Now tell me how much *you* want me,' he commanded throatily. 'Tell me.'

'I—'

The infuriating warbling of the telephone cut into the sweet, drenching pleasure of his touch, and Scarlett's eyes fluttered open to find Liam pulling impatiently at the knot on his hips which held the towel together.

'Let it ring,' he ordered huskily.

'I—can't.' I can't let him do this. I'll never recover if I do. 'Let me answer it!'

'No!' And his mouth began moving around to kiss her neck again.

Oh, God—what was she doing? It was probably her mother—worried sick after she had left her own engagement party and disappeared into thin air! The thought of her mother imagining the worst brought her to her senses more quickly than she would have thought possible, given the poundingly high state of her own desire.

'No!' she cried, and he went very still, his eyes almost black with sexual hunger. For one moment she half imagined that he was going to take no heed of her hypocritical request—a moment when she imagined him pushing her back down onto the bed until all her protestations had been kissed away and transformed into sweet surrender.

And you'd love that, wouldn't you, Scarlett? Blaming Liam for taking you by force, when it wouldn't be force at all...

But the moment passed without incident, and Liam made no move to stop her as she tore herself out of his arms and, without daring to look him in the face, rushed into the sitting-room and picked up the receiver.

'Hello?' she said.

It *was* her mother. 'Scarlett! Thank God! Where the hell are you?'

'I'm at home, Mummy,' Scarlett answered automatically. 'You just called me, remember?'

'Don't be so flippant! I've been going out of my head with worry. No one knew what to make of it!'

'I'm sorry, Mummy—I wouldn't have worried you for the world.'

'What are you doing in the flat? How did you get there?'

Where do I begin? she wondered in desperation. 'It's a long story,' she sighed.

'It had better be a good one!'

'Mummy, please don't nag—I'll explain everything.' But how? she wondered briefly.

'Well, you'd better speak to Henry.'

Out of the corner of her eye Scarlett saw Liam wander into the room, re-knotting the wretched handtowel which, given his current state of arousal, was now stretched almost to ripping-point over his hips. He saw her looking, raised his eyebrows a fraction, and her cheeks flared up hotly.

'Go *away*!' she mouthed. He completely ignored her, just carried on standing half-naked in front of her, a glint in the hatefully smug blue eyes. The sight of him looking like that would have tempted a saint, and she deliberately turned her back on him.

'What did you say, Scarlett?'

'Mummy—I'm running a bath.'

'Then turn the tap off.'

'I *can't*. Listen, I'll explain everything—but not now. And I'll ring Henry tomorrow.'

'Darling—you aren't having second thoughts, are you? About Henry, I mean?'

Scarlett paused. She wished that Liam would get the hell out of here and stop eavesdropping. He didn't even have the decency to *look* as though he wasn't listening! 'I can't talk about it now,' she said carefully. 'I'm a bit tied up. Just tell him not to worry, that I'll be in touch. And you're not to worry either. I'm *fine*. Honestly!'

'You don't sound fine,' said her mother doubtfully. 'You sound sort of—I don't know. Wild. Odd. Humphrey's furious with you.'

'He'll get over it.' It was thanks to Humphrey that she was being forced into this whole ridiculous charade—if Humphrey's feelings were wounded then it was just too bad. If he'd shown a little more business acumen then Liam wouldn't be in this impossibly powerful position. 'Please don't worry. I'll ring you tomorrow. Goodbye!'

'But—'

Scarlett replaced the receiver with a shaking hand and Liam came up behind her, so close that she could feel his warm breath on the back of her neck.

'Were they angry?' he asked casually.

'Of course they were angry! What did you expect? The last time they saw me was at my engagement party, when I left the room to get a breath of fresh air. Then I disappeared—quite literally. Humphrey's especially furious.'

'He would be,' came the sardonic reply. 'We all know that Humphrey feels he can be as unscrupulous as he likes as long as everything looks good on the surface.'

Scarlett let her head hang, feeling suddenly out of her depth, as though a chink had appeared in the blank screen of the future and she had glimpsed something nebulous and frightening which lay ahead. Something which Liam had triggered off and which could have no satisfactory conclusion. A future without Liam. But that was stupid—she *wanted* him out of her life.

Didn't she?

'Go away,' she said quietly.

But he didn't. 'Shh,' he said, surprisingly gently. 'You're as tense as a coiled spring. Come here.' He put two strong hands onto her shoulders and began to massage them rhythmically, and the sensation of warmth and strength and movement was as wonderful as falling into a bottomless pit of feathers. Scarlett found all the tension washing out of her.

'Good?'

She could tell that he was smiling. Anticipating surrender...

'Now,' he whispered, in a rich, husky voice which just *dripped* seduction, 'just where were we before we were interrupted, Scarlett? Remind me...'

The temptation to do as he asked was pulling on her good intentions as insistently as the wind tugging a kite up into the heavens, but she forced herself to visualise the icy jets of the shower she was planning to stand under until she cooled down.

'Go to hell!' she stormed, and ran straight into the sanctuary of the bathroom.

After her shower she spent an hour soaking in the bath, hoping that he would have gone by the time she came out.

Just who do you think you're kidding? she asked herself in disgust as she felt her heart pound erratically when she heard him moving around. She hoped he'd steer clear of her study. But then she heard him playing some kind of jazz on the piano.

And where did he learn to play the piano? she wondered as she wriggled into a pair of jeans and put on a thick Aran sweater. She put a bit of make-up on, and by the time she came back out into the sitting-room it was to find Liam dressed in a similar pair of jeans and a thick black sweater which emphasised his broad shoulders.

Except for the modern-day clothes he looked like a nineteenth-century smuggler, she thought. She could just imagine him hauling great barrel-loads of brandy into dark and frightening caves with that impressively formidable strength.

He looked her up and down. 'That's better. That's more like the Scarlett I know.'

'Meaning?'

He shrugged. 'That dress you had on last night wasn't really you, was it? That's how I remember you—always in jeans. Or jodhpurs. You should have looked like a tomboy—but I'd never seen anything so sexily feminine in my life. You were so bloody spirited, so feisty. Riding around on that horse of yours, with your nose stuck in the air and that cute little bottom giving me the most erotic fantasies imaginable.'

Too painful to think about—those early days. She searched around for something to distract her from his words. 'Where did you get your clothes from?'

'I rang the hotel and got them to send them over.' His eyes narrowed as he nodded in the direction of her study. 'You've started painting again,' he said suddenly.

'I told you not to go in there!' she retorted. 'I didn't give you *carte blanche* to have the run of my flat—and for your information I've been painting for years!'

'Interesting,' he observed. 'You showed a marked lack of commitment when we were together.'

Because I was too blinded by my love for you; there didn't seem room for anything else. 'That was a long time ago, Liam. People change.'

He held her gaze with a long look, the cold blue eyes piercing her more deeply than any arrow. 'Do they?'

She swallowed, that disturbing feeling of being way out of her depth swamping her again. 'Yes, they do,' she said tightly.

'You should sell them,' he said. 'They're very good.'

She didn't bother enlightening him.

'You know, this—' He frowned as he waved his hand around the flat, which was clean and brightly decorated, but modest by anyone's standards— particularly if you compared it to Seymour House.

'It isn't at all what I expected to find,' he commented.

'Just what *did* you expect to find?' she snapped. 'A bordello?'

He laughed. 'Now, there's a thought! I expected something much bigger. Something far more lavish. Do you rent it?'

'That's a very personal question, Liam.'

'I'm a very personal kind of man.'

'As a matter of fact I own the flat.'

His eyebrows moved fractionally upwards. 'Oh? And how's that?'

She lifted her chin. If she told him to mind his own business, he would think that she was ashamed. And she wasn't. 'I inherited the money from my American grandmother.'

He nodded, and the corners of his mouth briefly twisted. 'Of course,' he said scornfully. 'I should have guessed. It still all comes very easily for you, doesn't it, Scarlett?'

She gave a nonchalant little shrug, refusing to let him rile her, because her legacy had altered her life for the better in ways she had never dreamt of— but that was none of Liam's business. She'd hate to spoil his bad opinion of her!

'And you spend your days working in a dress shop on what seems a very part-time basis,' he observed.

Wrong, Liam, she thought gleefully. 'You *have* been doing your homework,' she said innocently.

'Mmm.' The scornful smile became a derisory slash. 'So how, I wonder, do you fill in the rest of your time? Are you one of the "ladies who lunch"? Or do you simply "shop 'til you drop", as they say?'

Just as she'd thought! Well, let him retain his warped prejudices about her! 'Oh, absolutely,' she replied airily. 'I can't tell you how *exhausting* it can be!'

'I can imagine,' he said disapprovingly.

She remembered the mellow notes of music she had heard him producing. He hadn't played the piano when they'd been together. Just what else had he learned to do in all the years they'd been apart? Curiosity got the better of her. 'Where did you learn to play the piano?' she asked suddenly.

'In Boston.'

'*Boston*? I thought you said you lived in Australia.'

'I do. But I've travelled in the interim. I told you I'd been to the States.'

'And what were you doing in Boston?'

He glanced at his watch. 'It's a long story, which I haven't got time to tell if we're going to get you that visa. So grab your passport and get your coat on.'

'Liam—you don't mean this—'

'Get your coat on.'

He was about as flexible as a brick wall, thought Scarlett crossly as he proceeded to whirl her across London. First he took her to a travel agency and bought them both a first-class ticket to Perth for

the following day. Then he took her to Australia
House.

To her astonishment, she was informed that yes,
she could have a visitor's visa, provided she
fulfil all the necessary criteria. One of those criteria
was that she had a fairly hefty amount of money
in her bank account.

'But I don't—'

'Here is a bank statement of my wife's and my
current account,' cut in Liam smoothly as he
produced a buff-coloured envelope from his back
pocket.

Current account? Scarlett's eyes widened as she
saw the amount registered under the heading 'Mr
L.A. & Mrs S.A.V. Rouse.'

'Liam—' she began, but he put a benign finger
over her lips.

'Not now, sweetheart,' he said, in an infuriat-
ingly indulgent manner. 'This gentleman wants to
ask you a few questions.'

She got her visa within the hour, after they had
both satisfied the authorities that they were estranged, and that Scarlett had no intention of ap-
plying for residency. She could see that the
admitting officer looked slightly perplexed as to
why a couple who had been separated for ten years
were planning on spending a fortnight's 'holiday'
together, but then Liam took over, and managed
somehow to convince the official that she wasn't
planning to stay.

He took her to a pub for lunch.

'Since when did we ever have a joint account?' she demanded, when he'd brought two glasses of beer and a plateful of sandwiches over to their table.

'Since a couple of weeks ago.'

'It's stuffed full of money! Where did all that come from?'

'From me,' he said drily. 'Don't worry, Scarlett—I came by it perfectly legitimately. And I opened the account because I'm not expecting you to have to pay for the privilege of coming to Oz with me.'

'Some privilege,' she said moodily, feeling thoroughly steamrollered by the way in which he seemed to have taken over her whole life. 'I can't wait until this is all over,' she sighed as she took a half-hearted mouthful of a cheese and pickle sandwich she didn't really want.

But that wasn't true at all—not really. Because already, after less than twenty-four hours in his company, something had happened to her—something quite disturbing if she sat down and analysed it.

Because she felt really and truly *alive* again—as if someone had given her some amazing new herbal drink which had done everything it had claimed to do and totally revitalised her. She felt the way she'd done when they were young, when she'd thought that the world revolved around him. It was exhilarating and giddying and terrifying, because soon it would be over and she would be back to being just Scarlett again—that moderately contented but somehow one-dimensional woman. And God help her if Liam ever found out how she felt.

Well, she would have to make sure that he *didn't* ever find out.

But something else nagged at her subconscious too, an issue which she could no longer ignore, and she knew that there was something she needed to do before another second passed.

'I'm going home now,' she said suddenly.

'Finish your lunch.'

'I'm not hungry!'

'Well, I am. Let me finish mine and then I'll take you.' And he bit into his sandwich, looking irritatingly unperturbed.

'I don't want you to take me! I have to—to—speak to Henry. Tell him—tell him that I'm going to be away for a couple of weeks.'

The blue eyes glittered with some indefinable menace, as though he weren't used to having his wishes challenged. 'I *said*, I'll take you,' he reiterated angrily.

Simmering, Scarlett waited until he'd almost finished, without quite knowing why she was allowing him to ride roughshod all over her, but trying to justify it to herself in all kinds of ways. Because she didn't want to make a scene. Because she wanted him to leave her alone after all this was over, and if she put his back up then he might not.

Liar, taunted her conscience triumphantly. You know why you're letting him do this—because secretly you like Liam's control and power and mastery. You're nothing but a weak, weak woman who's crying out for his domination...

The hell I am!

'I'm going,' she said, and rose abruptly to her feet, but he was following her out of the pub and holding open the door of the car.

Still seething, Scarlett kept her eyes averted and wouldn't speak to him, and in silence they drew up outside her flat.

'What's the matter, Scarlett?'

She turned to him, her gold eyes sparking like a bonfire. '*You* are! I hate you! Your high-handedness! Your—'

He bent his head and silenced her with a kiss— a kiss fuelled by anger and frustration, which was unbearably exciting. He kissed her until she had no breath left, no thoughts but of him and the devastating effect his kiss was having on her. She moved restlessly in his arms as she felt his hand brush over her straining breasts, not caring whether anyone could see them, just wanting him to... to...

His voice cut into her thoughts like a lathe as he moved away from her. 'Not now, Scarlett,' he said drily. 'I'm a little too old for making love in cars— particularly in broad daylight.'

Her hand went up instinctively, and she slapped his face furiously, but he took the blow without flinching, an arrogant look of satisfaction written all over his face.

'By the way,' he said coolly, 'don't forget to mention grappling in the front seat of my car, will you, Scarlett?' And he gave her an insulting smile. 'When you speak to Henry.'

CHAPTER SEVEN

'WHAT did you tell him?'

Scarlett pretended to misunderstand Liam's growled question. 'Who?'

'The man whose bed you'll be sharing in five weeks.'

Guilt rushed through her as she thought about yesterday morning and which particular man had almost shared her bed then. 'Do you have to be *quite* so graphic?' she snapped. 'Is that all you ever think about?'

'What's the matter, Scarlett?' he mocked. 'Why so touchy? Does plain speaking offend you these days—or are you just showing a touch of pre-bridal nerves?'

'Oh, leave it alone, why don't you?' Scarlett turned her head and stared determinedly down at the large diamond solitaire which winked up at her like an evil eye. She sensed rather than saw Liam give her a sideways glance, and she deliberately moved her hand so that the sunlight flashed down onto the brilliant and sent dazzling rainbow rays to spill colours all over her lap. He gave a small snort, and Scarlett was jerked forward as his foot was slammed down onto the accelerator.

They were driving to the airport, again in the Porsche, which apparently was hired and which

Liam would leave at Heathrow. He had told her this with the casual air of someone to whom money was no object, as if he spent a lot of time driving expensive hire-cars and leaving them at airports. She supposed that he did. It was scarcely credible that her Liam—that wild and untamed man from her past—was now a powerful businessman with a controlling interest in a *bank*, for heaven's sake!

She tipped her head back against the soft leather of the seat and sighed. Over the last twenty-four hours she'd scarcely had time to *think*!

Everything had happened in such a rush, what with Liam rushing her around in that insistent way of his—buying tickets and acquiring visas—that she still hadn't managed to find out just exactly how he had effected this most dramatic transformation of his fortunes. Or rather, she had tried—once— but he had clammed up with that stubborn, tight-lipped look of his she remembered so well. I bet it *was* illegal, whatever it was, she thought maliciously, but the idea held not one iota of conviction.

'So what did he say?'

'Henry?' she queried sweetly. 'That's none of your business,' she prevaricated. He wasn't going to find out what Henry had said. Not now. Not ever.

She searched around for a change of subject. 'Are we nearly there?' she asked disingenuously. As they were passing underneath a gigantic neon sign which read 'Heathrow Airport' it was fairly obvious that they were, and she saw him fail to repress a smile, as if he had seen right through her. Exasperatedly she turned her head to stare sightlessly out of the window.

She had spent the morning wondering what would have happened if she had simply called his bluff. How would he have reacted if she had told him airily that Humphrey's financial problems were nothing to do with her?

Then she needn't have accompanied him.

And wasn't that the whole point? That she was bursting with curiosity to know what his life was like? She *wanted* to spend this fortnight with him. Shaming, but true. I might even manage to get him out of my system, she thought, without a great deal of conviction, as they walked together into the first-class lounge.

He was wearing the classic American look of black jeans and a white T-shirt, with a black leather bomber jacket slung over his shoulder. The simple outfit was a knockout if you happened to be tall, good-looking and without a hint of excess flesh. And Liam was all those. He could have been a male model, she thought reluctantly as she covertly watched him walk over to pick up a newspaper. Or a pirate. Or a rancher, she decided, her attention caught by the powerful width of his thighs.

'Such a dreamy look in those big, golden eyes.' His deep voice cut into her thoughts. 'What were you thinking about?'

She tried to imagine what he would say if she blurted out, Your muscular thighs, actually! She felt a blush stealing up the back of her neck.

'Getting a little hot around the collar, Scarlett?' he murmured, the glint in his eyes daring to suggest that he had a pretty good idea in which direction her thoughts lay. 'Why don't you take your sweater off?'

She glared at him as she pulled the cotton cable-knit over her head without thinking, and the raven hair which she'd loosely pinned up, because it had looked even straighter than usual, tumbled down in a cascade of jet all over her shoulders.

'Nice,' he murmured appreciatively.

Which was just what he'd said when his lazy finger had stroked her bare thighs... Oh, for heaven's sake! Now the blush had started up all over again. She was behaving worse than any teenager. And maybe that's always going to be the effect he has on me, she thought gloomily. Arrested emotional development where Liam Rouse is concerned. 'Can I have some champagne, please?' she asked.

'Sure.'

A stewardess appeared in answer to the milli-metre elevation of his left eyebrow, and returned minutes later with champagne for her, mineral water for him.

Scarlett gulped down the delicious cold bubbly more quickly than she had intended, and because it had the immediate effect of bolstering up her mood she gratefully accepted another one.

Liam frowned. 'Do you really think you need that? You didn't, as I recall, have anything for breakfast other than two cups of that disgusting coffee which you produced from I dread to think where.'

How could she have eaten breakfast after the second most disturbed night she'd had in ten years? She'd woken once and crept out into the sitting-room, befuddled and groggy, thinking that he would still be camped out on the sofa, but of course he hadn't been. He'd gone back to the Ritz that night, and she had frostily declined his teasing invitation to accompany him.

He'd arrived early to wake her up, looking all glowing and vibrant after an early-morning run. And she'd been too strung up to do anything but offer him a cup of coffee with a shaking hand. Coffee which he had tasted and then openly winced at.

'It wasn't disgusting! It came out of a jar, that's all! But I suppose instant isn't good enough for you!' she challenged, then took another huge mouthful of her champagne. If Liam thought that a second glass wasn't a good idea then she'd damned well have a third! He was so bloody calm, so unflappable—she found herself wanting to rile him and rile him, and see just what would happen if she made him snap.

He shuddered. 'Your coffee tasted like mud, Scarlett—too many years of other people making it for you, I suspect. But I'll make you some decent coffee some time.'

'I can hardly wait! And as for having other people making it for me—you seem to forget that

I've been living on my own for almost nine years now,' she pointed out.

'Ah, yes—your mysterious past.'

'Not half as mysterious as yours!' she retorted.

He gave the glimmer of a smile. 'Not to worry, Scarlett. We'll have plenty of time to get—er—reacquainted during the next couple of weeks.'

And just what did *that* mean? she wondered. She had a pretty good idea. Liam wanted sex with her, and her behaviour up until now must have made him pretty confident of getting it. Well, if so, he was in for the shock of his life!

'Although it *is* strange,' he mused, almost to himself, 'that while I have been going up in the world you seem to have taken a trip in the opposite direction. That flat, for example—a very surprising choice, Scarlett. Henry, too—not the kind of man I'd imagined you ending up with.'

'You mean, he isn't like you?' she challenged.

He gave a quirky smile. 'You flatter me.'

Oh, hell! 'Well, I didn't intend to!' she retorted. 'Though as a matter of fact perhaps you've hit the nail on the head. Maybe I did go for someone who was as unlike you as could be. Perhaps I was just ambitious to beat our outstanding record of a two-month marriage!'

'So what are you planning this time around—forty years of stability, otherwise known as deadening and stultifying boredom?'

She stared at him. 'You don't really know me at all, do you, Liam?'

'That depends,' he answered, his eyes half-closed, 'on how you define knowledge.'

Oh! How was he managing to twist round every-thing she said so that in the end it resembled some-thing completely different? 'I'd like another drink, please.'

'You don't need one.'

'Let *me* be the judge of that, Liam,' she said superciliously, and was rewarded with a black glare.

'I've a good mind to wipe that smug little smile off your face,' he said in an undertone.

'How?' she enquired, increasing the smirk.

'You know very well how,' he answered silkily.

'Oh, *Liam*!' She tutted. 'And destroy the dreams of every other woman in this lounge if they saw you kissing me?'

Now the smirk was his. 'Who said anything about kissing?'

She gritted her teeth behind the smile and widened her eyes hopefully at the stewardess, who brought her a third glass. But rather to her an-noyance Liam didn't raise another objection, merely picked up the pink pages of the *Financial Times*, leant back on the sofa, and started reading them with rapt interest.

Behaving badly kind of lost its kick when the person you were trying to irritate wasn't taking the slightest bit of notice of you. She *knew* that she was behaving badly, but she couldn't seem to stop herself. He didn't seem to have any regard for how *she* might be feeling.

He had just come waltzing back into her life as though nothing had happened, and had coerced her into going abroad with him. Was he totally insensitive to the fact that she had been heartbroken when he'd gone? Sitting waiting like a fool—waiting for him to come home again. But he hadn't come home. He had disappeared. The rat!

She sipped the champagne mechanically, and it didn't taste so good any more—more sour than dry—but she was determined to finish it. And still that dark head scanned the list of share prices as if it were the nation's top bestseller. Insensitive swine! Feeling more sorry for herself by the second, she beckoned the stewardess over.

She smiled brightly. 'Could I have another, please?'

But the stewardess's gaze seemed to be fixed slightly to Scarlett's left, and she turned a fraction, only to see Liam giving the stunning redhead a slight shake of his head.

'No more, thanks,' he told her.

'Certainly, sir.' The redhead gave him a conspiratorial smile, and wiggled her perfect bottom off to the other side of the lounge.

'You can't do that!' exclaimed Scarlett, wondering how the stewardess ever managed to sit down in that skirt, it was so tight.

'I just did.'

The world seemed suddenly to become terribly simple. And sad. 'I wouldn't be shrinking—I mean drinking—if you weren't being so horrible to me,' she sniffed.

'And am I being horrible to you?'

'Yes, you are! You know you are! Forcing me to go away with you like this.' Her voice quavered before she could stop it.

'A fortnight's not so very long, is it?' he soothed. 'Come here.' And he gathered her into his arms.

Oh, it was bliss. Scarlett struggled ineffectually. 'Let go!'

'Why? Don't you like it?'

'No!'

'Liar!' he murmured softly into her hair, and she blamed the champagne for letting her give up the struggle.

Getting onto the aircraft was all a bit of a blur. Scarlett vaguely remembered making some terribly witty remarks to the customs officer about being kidnapped, before Liam grimly almost picked her up and carried her onto the plane.

Then followed the longest round of meals, drinks and sleep imaginable.

Scarlett awoke to find herself slumped halfway across Liam's lap, with the captain announcing that they were shortly to commence landing at Perth Airport.

She stared up into a pair of bright blue eyes. 'Oh, heavens!' she exclaimed in horror, and, shifting her position, she scrambled up and hastily made her way to the loo.

'I've got a splitting headache!' she groaned on her return. She had tried to do a hasty repair-job to her face, using the minute mirror, but it hadn't worked.

'I'm not surprised, after the bucketful of champagne you insisted on drinking,' he commented, with an acerbic lack of sympathy.

'I know. I know. And if you say "I told you so!" I think I'll scream.'

'I wouldn't dream of doing anything so obvious,' he replied, completely unperturbed.

To Scarlett's surprise that was the end of the lecture, and he somehow managed to get her two headache tablets and a drink of icy water.

'Thanks,' she said as she took them gratefully, feeling an idiot of the first order.

'Feel better?'

'A bit.'

Scarlett peered out of the window with interest, at the brilliant sapphire glitter of the Indian Ocean—matched only by the sparkling of individual swimming pools, which it seemed that almost every house had.

After they had landed, there were passport and immigration officials to satisfy, until at last they were out of the airport and getting into a Range Rover.

'Make yourself comfortable,' Liam told her. 'We've a bit of a drive ahead of us.'

'Don't you live in the city, then?'

'I have an apartment in the city and a house to the north, by the Moore river.'

'And is that where you'll be entertaining these clients of yours?'

There was a short pause. 'That's right.'

Scarlett tucked her legs up on the seat beneath her, glad that she'd worn her most comfortable jeans. For a while she watched the sunshine-bathed scenery flashing by, catching sight of one of the famous black swans which Liam had told her to look out for on the Swan river, but gradually her eyelids grew heavy, and, her head falling onto her shoulder, she slept.

She awoke to the green lushness of a river basin, to Liam bringing the Range Rover to stop in front of a delightful two-storey house. It somehow wasn't at all what she had expected. It looked older than she had expected. Lived-in.

It looked . . . Scarlett found herself swallowing, and turning quickly to hide her head lest he see it. It looked exactly like a *family* home. Large, but not too grand, simple and freshly painted, without any fancy porticos—it was the antithesis of the house she had grown up in.

She loved it on sight.

She looked up to find him studying her reaction, the blue eyes hooded and watchful and all-seeing. She turned away to look at the garden, suddenly shy, not wanting him to detect any trace of vulnerability on her face as she stared at the kind of happy-looking house she had never had but had always wanted.

To the front was a surprisingly green lawn, bordered by lush-leaved shrubs with starry and sweet-scented blooms, which spilled with glorious and chaotic profusion onto the path—as unlike the formally laid-out gardens of Seymour House as it was possible to imagine.

It took very little for her to imagine a family living here—a little boy kicking a football around, knocking the tops of those self-same bushes, a small girl plucking blossoms from the flowerbeds with chubby fingers. She thought of the child they'd almost had, and tears started somewhere at the back of her eyes, but—thank God—Liam was now too busy pulling their suitcases out of the car to notice her foolishness, and by the time he was standing beside her she had composed herself enough to express herself in the safest of remarks.

'How on earth do you keep the lawn so green?'

He smiled. 'You imagined Australia to be all desert?'

To be perfectly honest, she'd hardly given her destination a single thought. 'Right.'

'Well, we get a very generous amount of rainfall in the winter, and we conserve what we can. My bathwater helps keep that lawn looking so beautiful!'

She laughed uneasily as he led her inside. Imagine! Liam owning a home like this, and caring about lawns and gardens and recycling bathwater. Suddenly she realised that there was very little left of the stubbornly proud young labourer who had used their grotty little flat as little more than a place to sleep.

Inside it was cool and shaded, and in the quietened light Liam suddenly seemed to have retreated, to have become some distant stranger—a man, perhaps, whom she had never really known, had never really had the time to know.

'I'll show you to your room,' he said.

'Thank you,' she answered.

Strange that he had gone all formal on her—funnily enough she almost felt safer when he was trying to get into bed with her! With that newly acquired coolly impartial mask it was impossible to tell what he was thinking—or plotting!

The house was deceptively large inside, and he led her to a room on the first floor.

He pushed open the door to a room which was charmingly decorated in different shades of yellow—from walls of palest primrose right through to cotton curtains of the deepest, brightest sunshine yellow. A painting showing a burst of sunflowers in a blue vase complemented the room perfectly. It was full of bright, clear light, and Scarlett looked around it with pleasure.

'What a gorgeous room!' she responded instantly.

His eyes were narrowed as they watched her reaction, as if it were in some way important to him. 'But very simple?'

She shook her head. 'Perfect.' She took her jacket off and threw it down on the bed, meeting his enquiring gaze with a steady one of her own. 'My tastes are my own, Liam, not my parents'. I'm no clone of them.'

'Do you think I don't know that?' he queried softly. 'Do you think I'd ever have married you if you had been?'

Scarlett blinked. Well, now—that *was* confusing. That was almost implying that there had been an element of free choice about it. But surely the only reason he had married her had been because of the baby?

'Are we here...?' Her voice tailed away, but disconcertingly he cut into her thoughts with pinpoint accuracy.

'All alone? Yes, Scarlett—I'm afraid we are.' There was a hint of dry amusement in the deep voice.

And I'm not afraid of that, am I? Determinedly she kept her questions on strictly neutral lines. 'But a house this size—how do you manage?'

He put her suitcase down. 'I spend weekdays in the city—I'm only here at weekends. I have someone to keep an eye on the garden for me while I'm away, and a woman from the nearby town helps with the cleaning. But no one living in—no servants,' he emphasised. 'I kind of had enough of that while I was growing up.'

Scarlett spun around, her patience snapping. 'Oh, for God's *sake*, Liam—have you still got that huge great chip on your shoulder? Do you still blame me for not being born the same as you—as if it made any bloody difference!'

But, to her surprise, he didn't retaliate in response to her outburst, merely shook his head. 'Not at all, Scarlett. I left any chips behind—real or imagined—a long time ago.'

Their eyes met, and she looked back down over the years and saw the twelve-year-old boy fuse into maturity onto the chiselled features of the man. I like him, she thought, with a sudden rush of liberation. I've always liked him, even when he most infuriated me. There's something deep and good and strong that runs at the fundamental core of the man. She gave a smile which was tinged with sadness. Why the hell couldn't I have met him now, instead of then?

And with this sudden enlightenment somehow came the courage to face up to the past, to stop running away from it as she'd been doing all these years, and she was filled with a desire to fill in the gap between then and now. 'So how did Liam Rouse come by all this?' she asked.

'Time for the life story, you mean?'

'Some of it I know,' she said, more softly than she'd intended. 'Up until twenty, that is.'

There was a moment's silence before he shook his head. 'Not now, Scarlett. You're too tired. It was a long flight and you're jet lagged. Why don't you get some rest and we'll talk over dinner?'

But some demon flared up inside her. The bed looked comfortable but uninviting, and she was too restless to be sleepy. 'I'm not tired,' she said stubbornly. 'I've done nothing but sleep since we boarded that plane!'

He smiled. 'Want to go for a swim?'

Scarlett's eyes widened. 'You mean you have your own pool— here?'

He laughed. 'It's no big deal. In Australia everyone has their own pool.'

'Whereas in England those who do can only use it for three months of the year!'

'Precisely,' he laughed. 'So do I take it that the answer is yes?'

'Yes!'

'Then grab your bathing suit and meet me downstairs in ten minutes.'

CHAPTER EIGHT

SHE met him downstairs as instructed. She was wearing a white-embroidered kimono over her black silk one-piece, while he stood waiting for her in dark trunks, a towel hanging round his shoulders.

He didn't say a word, just briefly scanned the satin wrap-over which came to mid-thigh, then motioned for her to follow him through the house.

The pool lay to the back of the house—a large but functional rectangle of glittering blue water with the sun beating down on it. No fancy kidney-shaped pools for Liam.

Scarlett remembered her engagement party on that dark, snowy night. Was that really only three short days ago? It seemed like a lifetime. The sun beat down on her bare head. 'It's like a different world,' she said, half underneath her breath, but he must have heard her for he nodded.

'It *is* a different world,' he agreed. 'A different life out here—much freer.'

She looked around at the riot of blooms and sniffed appreciatively at their heady scent. 'In what way?'

He shrugged. 'Here one has the chance to excel—but on your own terms, not on anyone else's.'

Goodness—how ruthless he sounded, thought Scarlett, and then changed her mind. No, not ruthless, exactly. He had spoken with a steely and uncompromising determination to succeed, and she supposed that there was nothing wrong with that. After all, men—as providers—had been ambitious since the world began.

'Couldn't you have done it in England?' she asked suddenly. 'Excelled, I mean.'

'Naturally.' There was the trace of an arrogant smile. 'It might have taken a little longer, that's all.' His eyes flicked to the inviting blue water. 'So what's it to be, Scarlett—a swim first, or the life story?'

Any more evasion and she'd go bananas! 'The life story,' she said firmly.

'Then why don't you sit down?' He pointed to the table and chairs which stood at the poolside. 'While I go and fetch us something to drink.' He tone was wry. 'I have the feeling you're probably very thirsty.'

Thirsty? She could have drunk the contents of the pool and still had room for seconds! She slipped her shades on and sat down in one of the big cushion-covered wicker chairs.

He returned a few minutes later carrying a tray; on it was a bottle of vodka and a pitcher of freshly squeezed lime juice over crushed ice, together with two glasses. He filled both glasses with the lime juice. Scarlett took one heavenly sip and then another, and watched while he added a shot of spirit to his own glass. She put her glass down on the table and turned to look at him.

'So?' she said expectantly.

There was a self-deprecating smile. 'You want to know how I made my money?'

Actually, that seemed less important than other things. 'And where you learned to play the piano,' she said curiously. 'And to love opera.'

He took a sip of his drink. 'It's easier if I start right from the beginning.' He put the drink down on the table, the sunlight turning it the colour of pale tourmalines. 'As you know, after...' He hesitated, but only fractionally, and a hard note came into his voice. 'After we split up I went to live in London.'

The dark clouds floated back into her mind. 'So Humphrey told me,' she said coolly.

He glanced up at her, his eyes unreadable. 'If this story is going to be punctuated by recriminations, we may still be sitting here tomorrow morning.'

She sighed. Sometimes quarrelling was more force of habit than anything else. And she didn't *want* to quarrel with him—hadn't they done enough of that to last a lifetime? 'No more recriminations, Liam. Or rather—I'll try.'

He smiled at that. 'I was still labouring, sending what money I could to my mother. When she eventually found herself a job, I decided to take a working holiday in Australia.'

'I thought—' she began, then thought better of it.

But the blue eyes were narrowed. 'Mmm? What did you think, Scarlett?'

'That you might take up your place at university?' she offered. 'Surely they would have let you defer for a year?'

He took a large swallow of his drink. 'Oh, yes—they would have let me defer, but somewhere along the line I seemed to have lost my enthusiasm. Along with my ideals.'

She knew what he was referring to. There was a breathless, fraught silence. Scarlett waited in vain for him to ask her the question which hung in the air like another great stormcloud between them.

'When I came to Australia I thought I'd found paradise. At first I did the classic beach-bum thing and worked on the beaches—I sold ices and drinks. Those first couple of years seemed just like one long holiday.'

She could imagine. Liam tanned and working on the beach. Hordes of bronzed Australian lovelies hanging onto his every word. And not missing her a bit. Without a word, she picked up the bottle and poured herself a shot of the vodka. She had been the one who had insisted on hearing his life story, and if that meant opening up wounds which were bound to be painful—well, she could hardly blame *him* for that.

There was a tight, faraway expression on his face as she witnessed his own remembered pain.

'Then I got news that my mother had died,' he said sombrely. 'And after that there wasn't any real point in going back to England. There was nothing left for me there.'

'Nothing left for me there'. The words echoed round and round in her mind like a recurring nightmare, and Scarlett had to concentrate with every fibre of her being not to hurl her glass of vodka and lime all over him. She knew that, for God's sake—there was no need for him to spell it out in letters six feet high!

'So I set off around Oz—taking what work I could, seeing the sights. I settled in Victoria for a couple of weeks, and then the unbelievable happened.' He grinned, and it was frightening how the years fell away. For a second—just one second—with that smile she caught a glimpse of the man who had picked her up and swung her round and round in his arms as they'd walked out of the register office after their marriage. He had been laughing that day too.

'On Christmas morning, while the rest of the country were eating their turkey on the beach, a mate and I went backpacking. We were bored, and not a bit interested in Christmas. Christmas was for families, and he and I were distinctly lacking in the family department.'

Behind the protective cover of her shades, Scarlett blinked furiously.

'Barney was climbing on some rocks when he lost his balance and slipped. One of the rocks came down on his legs, crushing him.'

'Was he OK?' asked Scarlett in alarm.

'Eventually. But he needed digging out. And while I was digging him free—' he gave a dry laugh '—I found a bloody great nugget of gold.'

Scarlett blinked. 'You *are* kidding?'

Liam shrugged. 'That's what the guy from the minerals department said. Apparently, the chances of stumbling on gold like that are—well, infinitesimally small would be an exaggeration.'

Trust Liam! thought Scarlett, with reluctant admiration. 'So you sold it and lived happily ever after?'

He gave her an impatient look. 'It was worth around three hundred thousand dollars, that's all.'

All?

He topped their glasses up with lime juice. 'Instead of selling it I used the money to take out a land-holding in the form of a mining lease. Later I sold the lease.'

Scarlett blinked again. 'I see. Thus increasing your investment, I presume?'

'Significantly,' he answered coolly.

'And then?'

'Then I invested the money in land and property, and I was fortunate enough to do so in just the right economic climate.'

Scarlett felt a little faint. What Humphrey wouldn't have done for a little of Liam's business acumen! 'Which brings us up to the present day?'

He shook his head. 'Oh, no. I didn't have a resident's visa, and besides—it still wasn't enough.'

'But you must have been rolling in it!'

'Not the *money*, Scarlett. Once I had that I realised how little it really meant to me. I found that I wanted to achieve my full potential—both

materially *and* intellectually. And so I applied to
go to Harvard Business School.'

'Good grief! And naturally—being you—you got
in?'

'What do you think?'

She sighed softly. 'That you did.'

'Did you ever doubt that I would?' he quizzed
softly.

If he'd told her that he'd flown a rocket to the
moon, she thought she would have believed him.
Liam, she realised, was the kind of man who was
capable of anything! She shook her head. 'No.'

'I graduated well, and got my green card. Then
I worked in Boston for some time and eventually
was head-hunted for a consortium here in Perth—
which I now own.'

'And which has bought up much of Humphrey's
property?'

'That's right.'

And if he hadn't done that, if he hadn't rein-
volved himself in their lives, then none of this would
ever had happened. She wouldn't have seen him,
wouldn't have had to rediscover that some feelings
just never died . . . 'But *why* Humphrey?' she asked
desperately. 'What good will it do you, owning all
that land in England?'

'Property in a highly developed Western country
is always a sound investment,' he said, in the bored
tones of the businessman spouting the obvious.

'But that's not why you bought from Humphrey,
is it?'

He studied her dispassionately for a moment. 'No.'

'Why, then?'

'I told you already, Scarlett.' He gave a half-smile. 'It was a need to satisfy my youthful vow for revenge.'

'For what he did to your mother, you mean?'

There was a pause. 'You could say that.'

'And is it like they say? Is revenge sweet, Liam?'

The pause was longer this time. She heard him expel a breath of air, almost on a sigh. 'That's the funny thing, Scarlett—it doesn't actually mean a damn thing.'

Scarlett stared at him, her golden eyes troubled. 'So why do it?'

'It's done,' he said with finality, and added some more vodka to both their glasses. 'So that's me. Now it's your turn, surely?'

But for Scarlett it wasn't just like swopping anecdotes; it went deeper than that. Much though she had tried to tell herself not to let him, Liam had occupied a great deal of her thoughts over the years. Perhaps she had been obsessed with him just because she hadn't been able to have him—in the way that the dieter could think of nothing but food—although something deep within her doubted this. But now the gaps had been filled in—like a partially finished painting now completed—and she needed a bit of time to realign the Liam she remembered with the man he'd now become.

Except that fundamentally, she realised, he remained the same. He might have got rich along the way, and picked up an education. He might have acquired culture, become mature, urbane and sophisticated—but underneath it all didn't he still have the very qualities which had attracted her to him in the first place?

And—apart from fancying him like crazy—it had been his strength which had drawn her to him in the first place. That and his thirst for life. Was there another man in the world she would have loved enough to run off and elope with, thus defying her stepfather?

No.

'Scarlett?'

She looked up to find him studying her, his gaze strangely intent. For a minute she forgot where she was. 'What?' she asked stupidly.

'Fill in the years for me,' he said softly.

Someone protect me from those soft blue eyes, she thought helplessly. She grabbed at her glass like a drowning man at a raft. 'Nothing so impressive as yours, Liam.'

He frowned. 'Don't be flip. I want to hear.'

Perception fizzled like a slow blaze in her mind. 'But some of it you know—must know, surely? If you've been buying in England, from Humphrey, then you must have heard things about me.'

'I didn't deal with Humphrey directly. Even he, I imagine, with his fervour for the best possible deal, might have baulked at the idea of doing business with his daughter's estranged husband. All I know is that after our split you went off the rails.'

And you did nothing to stop me, she thought bitterly, but she pushed her chin up. 'And weren't you jealous?' she taunted. 'Even a little?'

She saw his knuckles tighten.

'You were patently unhappy with me, and I had no intention of putting a stop to your very obvious enjoyment of a newly discovered single life.' His eyes glittered. 'You loved it, didn't you, Scarlett? Every damned paper I picked up there you were— always with a different man. Dancing as if your life depended on it.'

She stared at him. It had. If not her life, then her sanity.

He had pushed his chair back. 'Tell me, Scarlett, did you let them make love to you? One of them? Or every goddamned one of them?'

'Liam—' But he was advancing towards her with such a terrifying look of rage on his face that she trembled in the baking heat of the day. Rage, undoubtedly. And something else too... 'Liam!' she repeated breathlessly.

But there was no point in appealing to his better judgement. Scarlett could sense it, could see it with her own eyes. She had wondered what would happen when Liam snapped; well, now she was about to find out. 'Liam,' she whimpered helplessly, but he was upon her, hauling her to her feet, pulling her into his arms, his eyes sparking angry and hungry fire, nostrils flaring like an excited stallion.

'Don't "Liam" me,' he taunted, an undercurrent of silky menace darkening his tone. 'Save your breath for what's to come.'

She gasped as he crushed his mouth down onto hers. It was like being pushed over the edge of a cliff—beyond reason and beyond desire. Fleetingly she recalled the first time they had made love—then, too, there had been this kind of desperation, this kind of fierce hunger which was all-consuming.

But now there was fury and bitterness mingled with their passion. A fury that appeared to have been lying dormant in both of them, waiting only for some spark to ignite it. His because of the imagined lovers who were supposed to have possessed her. And hers because for too long she had been missing this... This... She felt an aching hotness between her thighs, felt his hardness pushing against the silky kimono.

'Liam!' It was the last muffled plea she made, for he seemed to come to his senses, and raised his plundering mouth from hers, stood staring down at the way she quivered and trembled in his arms. His eyes blackened as he lowered his mouth again, and this time used sweet seduction to rouse her.

She felt her lips parting of their own volition to welcome the moist invasion of his tongue, dipping back and forth into the hot, eager cavern of her mouth, and as they did so he snaked his arm around her waist and pulled her up against his body, so that he could push the full hard throb of his arousal into the apex of her thighs again and again, as if to demonstrate explicitly what he would like to be doing—what his tongue was so deliciously mimicking.

The melting in her loins overrode everything bar the urge, the *need* to give in to every latent fantasy she had ever nurtured about him—and there had been many, many fantasies over ten long years. She trickled her fingers down to encircle each tiny, flat male nipple, and only when she heard him groan deep in his throat did she torture him still further by moving them on, allowing them to glide down over the hair-roughened chest.

He had left her mouth now, his head dipping, pushing the kimono off her shoulders so that it slithered to a silky unnoticed pool at their feet. Her fingers were continuing their relentless journey, and at exactly the same moment as his mouth found the silk-covered insistent bud of her nipple Scarlett slid her hand underneath the waistband of his bathing trunks and boldly captured the gloriously silken rocky sheath of him, and curled her fingers around him possessively.

His head jerked away from her breast and he stood looking down at her, his eyes almost milky with desire. 'Dear God!' he exclaimed, and she saw his mouth curve into a predatory smile, felt him grow—impossibly—even bigger in her hand.

'So that's what you want, is it, sweetheart?' he enquired huskily. 'So eager. So beautiful. Is this how you want it? Like this?' As he spoke his own hand slipped down, to push away the thin barrier of her swimsuit which shielded that most intimate part of her.

He pushed her to the ground and stared down into her face, his fingers beginning to caress her with intimate delectation while with the other hand he started to slide his bathing trunks down over the rock-hard thighs, the formidable power of him springing shamelessly free as he did so.

'Tell me,' he husked. 'Tell me what you want, Scarlett.'

She lifted her hips in impatient plea. She wanted the impossible. She wanted him to love her, as she still loved him. He had never loved her—not then, and certainly not now. But this would do. This would have to do.

'You know...' She could scarcely get the words out. 'You know what I want.'

'Yes, I know. I know because I want it too—more than anything. *Anything.*' His voice deepened to an irresistible challenge. 'Oh, sweetheart,' he whispered. 'Let's make love.'

'Oh, yes,' she sighed. '*Yes.*'

He gave a low moan as the trunks were peeled down to his knees, and he was just lowering himself down onto her when they heard the roar of a car.

There was one brief moment when she thought that he was about to take her regardless—one moment when he lay in frozen motion, just poised to enter her, and then they heard the squeal of brakes.

He made a muffled imprecation, and then, with a speed and a presence of mind which Scarlett could scarcely believe, he pulled his bathing trunks back up, picked Scarlett up with ease and walked to the edge of the pool, where, with her still held tightly in his arms, he jumped them both into the cool blue water.

CHAPTER NINE

SCARLETT landed with an almighty splash as she fell into the cool, clear waters, tumbling right down into the muted turquoise light at the bottom of the pool before kicking her legs and swimming swiftly to the surface, where she encountered Liam, dark hair plastered to his head, a wry look on his face.

'What the hell did you do that for?' spluttered Scarlett.

'Could you think of a better way of cooling things down?'

'But what was—?'

'Shh,' he said softly. 'Someone's coming.' Then he raised his eyebrows in a rueful and positively X-rated look as he realised just what he'd said, before hauling himself out of the pool.

Scarlett watched as he shook the water from his bronzed body and roughly towelled his torso dry, aware then of the sound of the clip-clopping of high heels rounding the front of the house towards the patio. She pushed her wet hair back behind her ears and started swimming a slow and steady crawl down to the end. She might be *partially* cooled off—but not completely!

She was on the return journey when the owner of the heels appeared, and Scarlett stopped mid-stroke, treading water as she looked up.

Every man's fantasy was clip-clopping her way towards Liam. High heels might now be out of date, but this cookie obviously knew that they were the best way of emphasising a fabulous pair of legs, thought Scarlett with a suddenly sinking heart.

For a start the woman was blonde, and Scarlett—like brunettes the world over—knew that gentlemen preferred blondes. There was something about the way that male conversation dried up whenever a female with fair hair came into a room. Scarlett had witnessed it time and time again. And, what was more, this woman's hair was almost waist-length, *and*—and here came the crunch—it looked completely natural, bleached almost white by the sun.

'Hi, Liam,' came a soft and sexy Australian drawl.

Scarlett's eyes moved to Liam's face, which was wearing a small smile. And a bloody fatuous one too, she thought angrily.

'Hello, Kelly,' he replied urbanely.

'You weren't answering your phone.'

'It wasn't connected.'

'Oh?'

She obviously knew him pretty well to be interrogating him like the Spanish Inquisition, thought Scarlett, still silently treading water, her cheeks flaming as she tried to stop herself imagining what would have happened should the blonde goddess Kelly have happened upon them just a couple of embarrassing minutes later.

And then her heart sank even further. What if Kelly was his girlfriend?

Oh, he wouldn't. Not Liam. He surely wouldn't have been seducing her by the edge of his pool if he was involved with another woman?

But *wouldn't* he? Did she really know him well enough to be certain?

Besides, I am still his *wife*, she thought. Legally, at least, *I've* got the upper hand. Not that he's bothered to get around to introducing me.

'I've just got back from England,' said Liam. 'And I have company.' And he turned towards the water with something resembling a smile. So did Kelly.

Scarlett felt like a bit-player going into action. With as much dignity as she could muster she climbed up the side steps of the pool, the black silk of her swimsuit outlining every curve of her body.

Close up, she could see that Kelly had green eyes, as narrow and as slanting as a cat's. And far too much make-up, thought Scarlett.

The blonde looked at her, gave her the once-over, then ignored her completely and turned her green eyes back towards Liam.

She was wearing a cream silky halterneck which displayed her high, pointed breasts to perfection, and it was teamed with a brown suede mini-skirt which was little more than a pelmet. Her legs were bare and very brown, and Scarlett got an even better look at the high heels. They were in matching brown suede. I'm surprised they aren't white, thought Scarlett, with surprising venom.

'Meet Scarlett,' smiled Liam. 'Scarlett—this is Kelly.'

Scarlett. Just that. No mention of their joint marital status. Well, he wasn't getting off with *that*! 'Hello, Kelly,' she said pleasantly, then flashed her eyes at Liam. 'Isn't it a little *sexist* to introduce women just by their Christian names, Liam?' she enquired sweetly. 'I'm sure you wouldn't do it with men. It makes us—' she glowered '—sound a little like club hostesses.'

'I used to be a club hostess,' said Kelly coldly. She preened as she flicked a long strand of white hair back over her shoulder. 'That was before I went into modelling, of course.'

Scarlett maintained her smile. 'Of course,' she said placatingly. 'And I'm sure you were a very good one too.' She extended her hand. 'Scarlett Rouse,' she said. 'And I'm very pleased to meet you.'

'*Rouse*!'

It had achieved the desired response. That screech was really most unattractive, thought Scarlett, shooting a slanted glance at Liam, whose eyes were dancing.

'Yes, Rouse,' she said pleasantly. 'Didn't Liam tell you that he was married?'

'I thought he was divorced.'

'Kelly,' cut in Liam quickly, 'we only arrived back a few hours ago. Both of us are pretty jet lagged.'

'Surely you're not going to send me away without a drink?' purred Kelly. 'I *have* just driven from

Perth, and it *is* a very hot day. And I'm very interested to meet your—er—*wife*.'

Liam's hesitation didn't last for more than a second, noticed Scarlett. Did *nothing* faze him? 'Sure,' he said smoothly. 'Scarlett—do you want to go and get changed? Catch up on some rest while I see that Kelly gets some refreshment.'

Scarlett, who felt at a dripping and somewhat scraggy disadvantage next to the sleek Kelly, was about to agree when something in the blonde's dismissive little glance at her stirred up a powerful and atavistic possessiveness within her. They might have been separated for ten years. And they might be almost divorced. But he was still her husband, dammit—and up until a few moments ago he had been making love to *her*.

And, what was more, she might be a past fixture in his life, but surely he wasn't planning on ending up with someone as obvious as *Kelly*?

'I'm rather thirsty myself, Liam,' she replied, her eyes glinting with mischief as she sank down into one of the chairs and picked up her glass. 'Oops! All my ice is melted.' She held her glass out to him. 'It must be hotter than I thought.' She gave him a saucy smile which was intended to remind him of just how hot things really had been, just a few minutes ago.

His blue eyes flashed more brilliantly than the sunlight on the swimming pool, and it was obvious that he understood her none too subtle message perfectly.

'Then you must let me fill you up,' he said, perfectly straight-faced, and was rewarded with an incredulous glower before he turned to the listening blonde. 'Vodka-lime, Kelly?'

Pink glistening lips were pursed. 'Oh, goodness me—no! Plain lime juice is just fine for me—I find I really don't *need* artificial aids to enjoy myself, and alcohol's so-o-o fattening, don't you find, Scarlett?'

'Not really,' said Scarlett mulishly.

Liam retreated towards the house—reluctantly, thought Scarlett, from the set of those broad naked shoulders. Probably wondering just what they were going to talk about in his absence. In a way it helped to have the openly hostile Kelly breathing down her neck—at least it meant she didn't have to confront what had almost just happened between her and Liam . . .

'So how long are you staying in Australia, Scarlett?'

Scarlett stared into a pair of calculating green eyes. 'We haven't really decided yet.' Which was true, since she didn't know when Liam's prospective clients would be arriving. She noticed with dismay how easily that possessive little 'we' had slipped off her tongue. Don't get used to it, she warned herself. You may be in for a brief physical reconciliation with Liam, but that's all it will be. Brief. Very brief.

'Is that an engagement ring I can see?' asked Kelly, eyeing the whopping great diamond with unashamed interest.

'Mmm.' Scarlett held her hand up so that the jewel caught the light. 'Do you like it? Liam couldn't afford a ring when we were first married,' she confided.

'Fancy giving away my secrets like that,' came a deep voice accompanied by the chink of ice-cubes, and Scarlett blushed, aware that she'd been caught out—so carried away with the pathetic and possessive little game she was playing that she hadn't even noticed Liam walking up behind them.

Kelly gave a rather forced laugh. 'I can't believe *that*, anyway. I can't imagine Liam not being able to afford anything—Liam has success written all over him! Why, he insists on weekending in this old place—but you should just *see* his apartment in Perth! Well, he owns the whole tower, of course, but his is right at the top. The *penthouse* suite,' she almost drooled. 'You can see the whole city from his bedroom!'

Liam didn't appear to be listening, but Scarlett looked at the woman with ill-concealed disgust. Apart from the crushing remark about his bedroom, she seemed almost as turned on by Liam's wealth as by the man himself. Suddenly she knew that she couldn't tolerate another second of this torture.

She pushed her untouched glass to one side and got to her feet. 'I think I will take that shower after all,' she said steadily. 'Goodbye, Kelly—have a safe journey back to Perth.'

She received a cold smile in return. 'And have a safe journey back to England,' came the rather pointed reply.

She felt their eyes on her as she walked back into the house, and, once inside that quiet, cool interior, she ran upstairs to her yellow bedroom and unzipped her suitcase. She pulled out some underwear, and as she did so she heard the angry screech of car-tyres on gravel.

Unable to resist the urge to do so, she hurried over to the window in time to see a white open-topped sports car with Kelly at the wheel, her white-blonde hair spilling behind her like a candy-floss cloud, driving like a bat out of hell.

She heard the sound of angry footsteps mounting the stairs two at a time, and Liam burst into her bedroom, his face a fury.

'Didn't you ever learn to *knock*?' she hurled at him.

He ignored that. 'I think that you and I have some talking to do.'

All her cool flew right out of the window. 'That *woman*!' she accused him. 'Liam—how could you?' She affected the blonde's husky drawl. '"I can't imagine Liam not being able to afford anything—Liam has success written all over him!"' She glared at him, her breathing coming fast and unevenly. 'And as for her comments about "the *penthouse* suite"— why, she was positively *drooling*!'

'It's OK, Scarlett,' he cut in coolly. 'I think you've made your point crystal-clear—though you're in danger of overstating it.'

She wasn't going to be silenced just because it suited *him*. 'Liam—she's awful—'

'Whereas you, of course, have excellent choice in men! Take Henry, for instance. Personally, I can't imagine anyone who would—but you seem to have other ideas.'

'You don't even *know* Henry!'

'And you don't know Kelly!'

'Well, at least I haven't...' Her voice tailed off.

'Haven't what, Scarlett?' he asked interestedly.

'Nothing,' she said sullenly, furious with herself for almost having given herself away.

'Haven't slept with him—is that what you were going to say?'

Damn him and his perspicaciousness! But the dull flush of colour to her cheekbones must have given her away. She raised her head proudly, her golden eyes flashing with challenge. 'That's right,' she said quietly. 'I haven't.'

'And may I ask why?'

'Because Henry wanted to wait—not that it's any of your business!' Henry *had* been content to wait, but she wondered now, with a terrifying flash of insight, whether she had been the cause of that contentment.

She had not been stirred to life in Henry's arms, had not responded as a woman should respond to the man she loved. Oh, she might have kissed him and put her arms around him, but inside she had been like a block of ice, praying for a reaction which had never come, which she had stupidly believed might come one day, like the good fairy—after marriage, perhaps?

'And you wanted to wait too, did you, Scarlett?' came the silky question.

'Yes, I did!'

'But not with me? Never with me!' His eyes were dark with triumph. 'Not then, and not today. No such restraint there. And why's that, I wonder?'

She had fallen with ease into his trap. She scrabbled around for an answer. 'Because maybe with you that's all it is,' she challenged. 'Lust. *Sex.*' But just the very mention of the subject reminded her of how close they had just been, and her body stirred into sudden life again.

She felt her breathing grow shallow, her mouth go dry, and her eyes now flashed him a different kind of challenge. She realised that they were both still in their bathing suits, though now dry, and it didn't take much for her to know that Liam still desired her too. She could see that quite easily from the way he was standing.

He gave a cruel kind of smile as he acknowledged the challenge—his own eyes flickered briefly to her swelling breasts, which were sending out a message as clear as day. He looked into her face as he shook his head.

'Oh, no, Scarlett,' he said softly. 'We aren't going down that path again. I know what it is you want. You want me to start kissing you and to throw you down onto the bed and make love to you. And I want to do that to you. We both know that. Don't we?'

He paused, his glance drifting briefly down in the direction of his own body, and she saw him shift as if trying to ease the incredible tension. He looked up again. 'That would make it so simple for you, wouldn't it? You could abdicate all responsibility. You wouldn't have to think about what you were doing, or with whom.'

His voice deepened into a cruel, seductive caress. 'But it's not going to happen like that. When it happens you're going to know exactly who it is who's kissing you, exactly who it is pinning you to the mattress. When I'm deep, deep inside you I'm going to make you open those beautiful golden eyes and say my name. *My* name, Scarlett—and no one else's.'

She was trembling but it wasn't with the rage she knew she ought to feel. It was with indignation, because he was right—damn him! And it was with desire, pure and piercing, threatening to engulf her with such a stormy pull that for a minute she contemplated pushing *him* back on the mattress, wiping that smile off his face with *her* kisses, seducing him against his will until she had pushed all that hateful and arrogant reasoning right out of his brain and he was responding to her, pleading with her, saying *her* name—only hers!

Trembling, she forced herself to surface from the deep, dark waters of her erotic fantasy. He couldn't really have put his case more brutally, could he? Not a *mention* of affection, or any explanation about Kelly's role in his life. So was she prepared to simply toss her pride away and just *let* him seduce her? She was not!

'It isn't going to happen Liam,' she said coldly. 'Not like that. Not any way. Not at all. Leastways, only in your imagination.'

He folded his arms and tipped his head back a fraction, surveying her through slitted eyes, a complacent smile written all over those ridiculously gorgeous features. 'Oh, yeah?' he mocked.

She gave him a chilly stare. 'I'd like to shower now, if you wouldn't mind leaving. Then I'm going to sleep.'

'Sure.' He laughed softly. 'Sweet dreams, Scarlett!' And he closed the door quietly behind him, leaving nothing but the trace of that deep, mocking laugh.

She rushed into the bathroom, throwing herself under the punishing ice of a cold shower which flooded over her hot and frustrated body like a benediction.

Oh, *why?* she asked herself despairingly. *Why* had she behaved like that? Why had she so easily almost let him make love to her? And if that wasn't bad enough why had she then enacted that pathetic little charade of them still being together in front of his girlfriend?

But even as she asked herself those questions she wondered if she would have the honesty to admit the truth.

The truth was that she loved him. She had never stopped loving him, and that was why she couldn't marry Henry—or anyone else for that matter. Because the only man she wanted to marry was her husband, and in a few short weeks he would no longer carry that status.

She worked dewberry shampoo into her thick black hair, lathered every centimetre of her skin with the same fragrance, then began to dry herself with one of the big buttercup-yellow towels.

If the truth were known she really couldn't care less about Humphrey and the perilous state of his business affairs. In her opinion her champagne-swilling, gambling snob of a stepfather deserved everything he had coming to him.

Instead she had come out here *pretending* that she wanted to help Humphrey, when all she wanted was to be back in Liam's life. For good.

And it was pretty plain that he wanted her back in his bed. But only temporarily. Why, he'd even bought her a return ticket!

I can't do it, she thought suddenly as she sat down in her bra and panties in front of the dressing-table mirror. I've changed. And what he's offering me is just not enough.

At eighteen she had been prepared to tolerate the one-sidedness of their relationship. It hadn't *mattered* that she had loved him totally and that he hadn't loved her. She had stupidly and foolishly — with all the naïveté of youth — believed that she'd had enough love for both of them. But even then, Liam had been mature enough to know otherwise.

She remembered the words he had spoken as though it had been yesterday — 'You only *think* you love me.' Hadn't that been his diplomatic way of telling her that it wasn't going to work? And it would have died a natural death if she hadn't trapped him into a marriage which could have ruined his life. Yet Liam had managed—incredibly—to overcome all the odds which had been stacked against him. He was an extraordinary man.

And she realised something else, with a hurt which drove a knife right through her heart—that she was part of Liam's revenge. Bedding her, making her respond with pleasure in his arms again before dumping her—wouldn't that be sweet revenge indeed for the price he had almost paid because of her deliberate seduction of him?

She glanced down at her watch. It was almost seven o'clock and she was tired. As tired and as weary as she could ever remember feeling, but strangely enough a weird kind of peace had enfolded her.

Because her life wouldn't have to be a pretence any more. She needn't worry about settling down and having babies with a man she'd tried to feel something for but couldn't. If she couldn't have Liam, then she didn't want any fourth-rate substitute.

And, besides, it was no big deal. She still had her painting. She had her own life in London. There were the parks and the theatres and the museums. These days you didn't have to rely on a man for happiness. It was a bonus if you met one and she had just been unlucky—it had been a case of bad timing.

Still in her bra and panties, she slipped beneath the cool butter-coloured sheets, her head sinking gratefully down onto a feathery pillow. She just lay there for a moment, watching the rays of the sun dancing on the milky ceiling. She yawned again. I'll tell Liam, she decided. I'll tell him that I'm not staying. I'll tell him later—at supper.

But when she awoke she could sense immediately from the glaring quality of the light that it was morning. She picked up her watch from the bedside locker and looked at it. It was almost ten o'clock.

She pushed the sheets aside and went out to the bathroom, brushed her teeth and brushed her hair. She'd gone to sleep with it damp and it had dried into an annoying kink—but what the hell? She wasn't trying to impress anybody, that was for sure. She stared at her face. Amazing. It had the faintest glow of colour to it, and that was just after an afternoon by the pool.

She felt her cheeks grow warm as she remembered what had happened—or rather what had *almost* happened—but then pulled her shoulders back with renewed resolve. What she had decided last night seemed even clearer in the cold light of morning. She wasn't staying here a minute longer than she had to.

There was a light rap on the door.

'Come in,' she said hesitantly.

It was Liam, carrying a breakfast tray. He was wearing faded blue denims and a white T-shirt. 'See—' he smiled '—I knocked.'

'Liam—'

'Scarlett—I'm sure that you want to harangue me, and to tell me things which are no doubt very important, but you're not going to do it on an empty stomach.'

'But—'

'No buts,' he said firmly. 'You had no supper. You're to eat something and drink some of my superb coffee—which you once told me you couldn't wait to drink.'

'I was being sarcastic, actually.'

He grinned. 'And they say there's a lot of truth in sarcasm. Now, why don't you hop back into bed?'

There was an odd note to his voice, something in the way he was avoiding directly looking at her, and she suddenly realised, to her dismay, that she was wearing nothing but her white cotton bra and pants! She leapt beneath the covers faster than an Olympic sprinter, and watched while he poured out two cups of—admittedly—the most fragrant coffee she'd ever smelt.

She drank two cups, and hungrily ate the crusty bread coated with butter and thick honey while he took his own cup over to the open window and sat down on the ledge, very still and very silent.

She had finished her plateful of chilled berries when he turned round and smiled at her, and she had to steel herself to look back at him. This is temptation, she thought. Temptation in that smile, in the deceptive blueness of his eyes which can sometimes fool you into thinking that they have softened. This was much harder in its way to resist than his kisses, for that smile could mimic affection quite cleverly—and Liam's affection was still what her pathetic heart cried out for.

'I want to go home,' she said abruptly.

But he didn't look a bit surprised, merely nodded his head. 'Yes. I thought you'd say that.'

'You can threaten me with ruining Humphrey if you like, but I won't change my mind—that's between you and him. I'm very sorry if you're going to lose out on your business deal, but somehow I doubt whether that will hinge on *my* being here. I suggest that you use Kelly instead—I'm sure she'd just *love* to play hostess for you.' She met his unwavering gaze. 'And if you try and keep me prisoner then I'll manage to escape somehow—and go to the police!' she ended dramatically.

He elevated the dark slashes of his brows with an amused look. 'Scarlett, Scarlett!' he remonstrated. 'What have I told you before about that imagination of yours? Can you really imagine me keeping you here against your will?'

'Yes, I can,' she said stubbornly.

He grinned. 'How? Locked in my bedroom? Chained to my bed wearing nothing but your pretty underwear? Awaiting my all too frequent visits with foreboding and...with...*pleasure*. Is that your fantasy, Scarlett?'

'Stop it!' Scarlet-faced, breasts tingling, she clapped her hands over her ears, and would have flounced out to the safety of the bathroom if she hadn't been so indecently dressed. 'I'm not joking, Liam. I want to go home.'

His face was suddenly sombre. 'I know you do. And go home you shall. But it can't be today.'

'Why not?'

'Because we need to get your ticket changed, and there are a limited number of flights from Australia to London. I doubt we'd get you on today's. But we can drive into the city, if you like, and book you on tomorrow's flight.'

'Thank you,' she said stiffly.

'So why don't you get dressed? I'll wait downstairs.'

She sat staring at the door as it closed behind him. She wasn't disappointed—she *wasn't*! And it wasn't as though she'd expected him to get down on his hands and knees and beg her to stay, was it?

Of course not.

It was just that she hadn't expected him to agree *quite* so easily, that was all. And she'd thought that he might at least try to kiss her, so that she would have had the pleasure of fighting him off and regaining the upper hand.

Still. She looked around the room as she headed for the shower. At least she hadn't unpacked.

She dressed in black jeans and a big crimson silk overblouse. She washed her hair in the shower, so that the kink disappeared, and let it hang loose and black and silky.

She was in the process of zipping her soap-bag into her hand-luggage when she was alerted by the sound of some birdsong she'd never heard before. She wandered over to the window, where Liam had sat earlier. There was no bird that she could see—

perhaps they were too well-camouflaged—but she stood for a moment looking down onto his paintbox of a garden, with its tall trees and the scented chaos of its shrubs.

It's peaceful, she thought. Quiet and beautiful and peaceful. In her mind's eye she allowed herself one blissfully sweet moment of fantasy—living here, with Liam, raising their children...

She turned away to pick up her bags, the image evoking more pain than she could bear, and made her way out of the yellow room.

He was waiting at the foot of the stairs, and he immediately came upstairs to take the bags from her.

'Let me.'

'I can manage,' she said ungraciously.

'*Scarlett*.'

She let him take them, though she didn't want him to. There was something about a man carrying your cases, something protective that made her feel all defenceless and womanly and *stupid*. Especially stupid as he was carrying them to put her on the first flight out of the country!

And he might, she thought viciously as she stole a look at the impassively handsome features of his profile, he might feign a *little* disappointment at the fact that she was going.

They drove back into Perth, and Scarlett, less sleepy than when she'd arrived, was amazed at how tall and clean and glittering and spacious it all looked.

The ticket was changed for the following day's flight without any trouble, and Scarlett sat moodily reading a magazine while Liam completed most of the paperwork. With a smile, he came over to the small table where she sat.

'All done. You fly tomorrow at twelve.' He glanced down at the discreet gold gleam at his wrist. 'We've time for some food. Come on—it's lunchtime, and I'm hungry. I'll show you the best restaurant in Perth.'

'I—' She opened her mouth to say that she wasn't hungry, but thought better of it. If *he* was going to be totally unaffected by this their final parting, then she could at least pretend to be the same. 'Lovely,' she smiled, praying that he didn't realise what an effort she was making not to howl into her handkerchief. 'But will they let you in looking like that?'

'Looking like what?' His eyes surveyed the clinging white T-shirt and the equally clinging jeans, and he grinned. 'Oh, you mean, dressed casually?'

Scarlett laughed in spite of herself. '*Casually*? Is that what you call it?'

'Sure. You don't need a stiff shirt collar and a blazer out here to look casual. This is Australia, not England.'

It was a pity, she decided as he negotiated the car through the traffic, that she was leaving before she could get a chance to know this vast and beautiful country which seemed to stand for everything that Liam loved. Because the more she saw, the more she liked it too. It was unpretentious, and sometimes brash, but it had a big, big heart. Or so Liam told her during the ride to the restaurant.

'People work damned hard out here, but they make up for that in their leisure. They play hard too.'

And the blue sweep of the ocean dazzled her as he parked the car.

The restaurant was perched above a sandy beach, and they sat outside underneath a shaded canopy, where a riot of waxy leaved plants displayed their dark green foliage.

Scarlett scanned the menu she'd been given, then looked up again. 'What do you recommend?'

'The fish.'

'Liam—it's *all* fish!'

'In that case I'd have the garlic prawns, followed by the crayfish—it's the best in the city.'

They placed their order and were given a bottle of superb Australian Semillon, which Scarlett sipped appreciatively.

'Good?' he queried, his blue eyes surveying her over the rim of his glass.

'It's out of this world.'

Was it because she was soon going that all constraints seemed to have flown during that wonderful lunch? The most delicious lunch she had ever eaten in her life.

She saw Liam in a new light that day—very relaxed, very much at ease in the laid-back but distinctly upmarket restaurant, where he was obviously a well-known and valued customer.

And Scarlett responded in kind, even managing not to dim her smile when two women stopped by their table to chat. Liam introduced them, but Scarlett scarcely took their names in, she was too busy trying to notice whether either of them was displaying the kind of body language which could indicate that she might be Liam's lover. True, he had Kelly—but that didn't stop him having others. She had no idea about his views on fidelity these days, and he was a free agent after all.

The meal finished, they sat and drank their coffee while Liam pointed out some of the sights which could be seen from their vantage viewpoint. Eventually he pushed his tiny cup away and surveyed her thoughtfully.

'What would you like to do this afternoon?'

She fidgeted awkwardly with the silver bangle at her wrist. 'You don't have to stay. If you would just take me to a hotel, I could—'

'Scarlett,' he said softly, 'don't.'

She stared across the table at him, her golden eyes puzzled. 'Don't, what?'

'There's no need for you to book into a hotel. I have a flat in the city.'

'You can see the whole city from his bedroom.' Kelly's gloating words floated back to torment her. Tell him you don't want to stay in his flat. Insist on a hotel. But the words refused to be spoken, and she didn't dare question why.

'And there's no need, you know, for us to part as enemies,' he continued. 'Is there? Why don't we have this one last day together—as friends?'

She felt as though the hangman had slipped the noose around her neck. Like a condemned man being granted one wish. And her wish—that Liam would suddenly and miraculously fall in love with her—was never going to come true.

But the smile she gave him matched his in brilliance—she really was becoming a most *commendable* actress. She nodded her head. 'That suits me fine,' she said, and he gestured for the bill.

They jumped straight down onto the beach to walk off the excesses of their lunch, setting off over the hot sand.

They walked in silence for a while, Scarlett hearing nothing but the hypnotic sound of the waves pounding in their age-old rhythm. She deliberately blotted her mind clear of all thoughts, enjoying this temporary calm, not wanting to speak lest she spoil it, and Liam seemed content to do likewise.

They walked a good distance before turning around to go back, and had almost reached the point where he had parked the car when they first heard then saw some commotion out to sea.

A small boat had apparently capsized, and someone was in trouble in the water. They stopped to watch the lifeguard swing into action. He was aged about nineteen—all bronzed solid muscle as he ran quickly towards the shore. But for the light brown colour of his hair it could have been Liam at the same age, thought Scarlett as they watched him strike out in a strong crawl. He must have been almost that age when he'd first come over here.

They saw a head bobbing in the water, one arm flailing wildly, and they watched while the lifeguard's powerful stroke gradually decreased the distance between him and the stricken vessel. After a minute or two he reached it, then disappeared momentarily out of sight.

It was Liam who first sensed that something was wrong. She felt him stiffen by her side and turned to look up at him, perplexed by the intent look on his face as he shaded his eyes with his hand.

'What is it?' she asked, but he was already kicking off his shoes and tearing off his jeans before running towards the water.

'The lifeguard's in trouble!' he shouted towards a group of teenagers who were sitting by the water's edge, just watching—for all the world as though they were at a cinema. 'There are two of them in the water! Can somebody *help* me?'

He dived into the water without waiting to see if anyone obeyed his instructions, but to Scarlett's everlasting relief one of the youths ran towards the water's edge in Liam's path.

She ran down onto the hard, wet sand, where the deceptively capricious-looking waves lapped innocuously.

And out there, she thought, her heart in her mouth, out there is Liam.

Suddenly whether or not he loved her seemed ridiculously unimportant. What if he died?

He couldn't *die*.

Unimaginable to think of all that vibrant life being snuffed out.

She screwed her eyes up against the glare of the water as she stared out to sea, watching—just watching—while fate held Liam's future in her fickle hands.

She saw his dark head reach the boat, then it too bobbed out of vision. The youth reached it seconds later. Scarlett looked around in desperation. Surely, *surely* there must be some other swimmers—something she or anyone could do? Yards away, hanging on a white post, she spotted the welcoming crimson of a lifebelt, and she ran to unrope it from its stand. It was surprisingly heavy, and she ran back with it to the water's edge, her eyes anxiously scanning the waters around the boat. Of the four in the water she could see no one, and she closed her eyes in sick despair.

Then she heard a shout. One of the teenagers close by was pointing, and to her immense joy she saw Liam's dark head. He was propelling an inert form through the waves, and, following close behind, the teenage swimmer was struggling to help bring the lifeguard in.

Scarlett felt suddenly and exceedingly impotent. She didn't know where to find a phone—she didn't even know the emergency code, for God's sake.

Her eyes staring wildly, she turned to the group beside her. 'Someone go and get an ambulance!' she shouted. '*Quickly*!'

One of them ran off, and Scarlett ran into water which foamed up to her knees towards Liam, seeing at once that her lifebelt wouldn't be any help to him at all. She threw it back onto the beach as he picked up the limp form of a young woman and carried her effortlessly out of the water before lying her on the sand.

His face was a white mask of despair. 'She isn't breathing,' he grated, falling to his knees beside the slack body. 'Her heart's stopped.'

Scarlett ran over and crouched down beside him. It had been a long time since she'd done this sort of thing.

Her fingers felt for the carotid pulse in the neck. Nothing. She gave one sharp blow to the sternum, then she moved to extend the girl's neck, bent her head and gave one long blow of air. 'See to the lifeguard!' she shouted at Liam. 'I can manage here!'

She heard him running across the sand while she continued with her lifesaving routine. Four pumps on the chest to a long blast of air. Please, she prayed silently while she worked. Oh, please.

She felt the girl's return to life as gentle yet as unmistakable as a breeze on a summer's day, and she quickly turned her head to one side—just in time, as the girl began to vomit up sea-water.

She heard the clamour of voices then, deeper, authoritative male voices, but she was so intent on holding the girl's stomach and forehead so that she could be sick, and thrilling with delight when she saw a pair of confused brown eyes open to blink up at her, that she wasn't aware that the ambulance had arrived until she felt a man's hand on her shoulder and looked up to see the welcome sight of the paramedics.

'You did well, love,' he said. 'We'll take over now.'

Scarlett had scrambled to her feet to look around when she felt two hands go round her waist from behind, and she whirled to look up into Liam's smiling face.

'The lifeguard?' she quizzed anxiously.

'Is fine. As, so I gather, is the girl. Thanks to you.'

'And to you,' she said quietly, the realisation of what had just almost happened beginning to hit her.

The world swayed, then misted over.

'Oh, Liam! Liam!' she cried, and promptly burst into tears.

'Hey,' he said softly as he gathered her into the warmth of his embrace, and she heard the wonderfully loud thundering of his heart beating out its exuberant rhythm of life. '*Hey*! This isn't the kind of reaction a man expects when he goes off to perform a heroic deed!'

She smiled through her tears. He was alive! 'Thank God!' she whispered, before she fainted.

CHAPTER TEN

'HERE.' The doors of the lift pinged open and Scarlett followed Liam into the penthouse flat she'd heard so much about. He guided her through a sitting-room the size of the Albert Hall and gently pushed her into a bathroom.

'First,' he said firmly, 'a shower.'

She turned to look at him. The invitation was there in her eyes. Death—or near-death—had an uncanny way of putting life into perspective.

He read the look correctly, and shook his head. 'No, Scarlett, you'll have to soap your own back—because I'm not getting into the shower with you. There's too much between us that has to be sorted out one way or another. If we *do* make love then it has to be on terms which are acceptable to both of us.'

And she could just imagine what *they* were. How many variations on 'no strings' were there? 'You chop and change your mind a lot, don't you, Liam?' she challenged fiercely

His eyes glinted. 'So I do. And perhaps the reason is that you have me so I can't think straight. The trouble with you, Scarlett, is that I start out with great intentions to talk things through, and somewhere along the line things always seem to get out of hand.'

She leaned back against the door. 'How?' She pouted deliberately, but he pushed her inside and closed the door.

'Ten minutes—that's all you've got. I'll put your clothes on the bed.'

Clothes? *Clothes*? The last thing in the world she wanted were her damned clothes! She wanted to be completely naked with Liam on some bed somewhere, to kiss every inch of him and be made love to with his inimitable thoroughness over and over again. Something to remember him by...

During those few unbearably long minutes while she had waited for Liam to emerge from the water things had fallen clearly into perspective for her. She knew he didn't love her, and of course that made her sad—but she could think of something which would make her a lot sadder. If she was consigning herself to a lifetime of celibacy then she wanted one more time with Liam. One long night to remember. And if that was wrong—well, then it was wrong. Tough! She didn't care. This was the beautiful feast before the fasting began. This was her reward—or her punishment.

She deliberately took longer than the ten minutes he'd assigned, but, to her chagrin, he didn't come in to find her. And when she emerged she saw that he had indeed put her bags out on the bed of what was obviously a guest-room, because it looked down over a vast and obviously communal swimming pool, where people lay on loungers, sunning themselves and sipping drinks.

As Scarlett dressed, in a white body with matching white jeans and a green silk overshirt, she felt sorry for every one of those people down there. Poor them! she thought. While they were lying there, seemingly enjoying the sybaritic pleasure of the good life, *she* would be spending the rest of the afternoon—and evening—and night—in Liam's bed.

After their 'talk', of course. She wondered what exactly it was that he wanted to say. She could imagine. Something on the lines of 'I'm not really looking for involvement, not at this time'. Or 'It didn't work out last time, so...'

She pushed the door open and wandered into the sitting-room to find Liam sitting there, a tea-tray in front of him. He had obviously used a different shower, since his hair was all damp. He'd put on clean jeans and a blue silk shirt. Little Boy Blue...

'Come and sit down.' He patted the seat next to him. 'Tea?'

'Please,' she answered, rather faintly. This wasn't what she had envisaged at all. She'd imagined his lips moving all over her body by now, but instead he was pouring some fragrant-smelling tea into an exquisite bone-china cup. He dropped a piece of lemon into it and handed it to her.

'Thanks,' she said in bemusement.

They sipped in silence, and in fact it was just what she needed. There was something so terrifyingly *normal* about a cup of tea. No wonder they gave it to shock victims.

When they'd finished they both put their cups down in front of them, then he turned to face her and she looked at him expectantly and closed her eyes.

'Open your eyes, Scarlett,' he said sternly. 'I want to talk to you.'

'Oh, talking, talking, talking!' she muttered. 'What good did talking ever do?'

'*Our* problem was that we never talked at all.'

'That was then. This is now.'

'And we're *still* doing it. Do you realise that our lunch today was the first time we've ever sat down as adults and talked like adults, instead of ending up in bed together?'

'Well, maybe that's because it's the first time we've ever been in a restaurant together.'

He sighed. 'God! So it is. Scarlett—' his voice was sharp '—where did you learn to do that?'

'What?'

'Lifesaving.'

She pursed her lips. 'Oh, it proved a very popular party-piece on the social round!' she said airily, but he gripped her arms with his hands.

'I mean it!' he ground out. 'Be serious for a moment, can't you?'

She pulled away from him. She might have known that this would happen. They would talk, they would start arguing—it would be exactly the same. 'Well, what do you expect me to say?' she demanded. 'You've got this image of me as the poor little rich girl, frittering her life away on the dizzy round of the social world. You were so keen to show me that *you've* changed—where on earth did you get the arrogance to presume that my life would have stayed static?'

'But I *have* tried to find out!' he exploded. 'And every time I ask you about it you retreat like a snail into its shell and refuse to tell me anything. What's the big mystery?'

'There's no big mystery. I just couldn't see the point of telling you, as our reacquaintanceship was going to be so brief.'

'So where did you learn it?' he persisted.

'I went abroad for two years. I joined the WAO—'

His eyes widened in disbelief. 'That's the World Aid Organisation?' he queried. 'Flies in foodstuffs and medicines to the Third World?'

She nodded. 'Yes. There were people there more qualified than me, but I had something to offer which made me invaluable—I was financially independent, thanks to my grandmother's legacy. It was the first time I've ever been pleased to have an inheritance. They insisted that I learn some basic first aid before I went out there. I can even deliver a baby,' she said proudly, before her mouth crumpled a little as she realised that she had strayed into forbidden territory.

'Can you?' he asked thoughtfully, as if he hadn't noticed. 'And what did you do when you got back?'

'I still work for them,' she explained. 'Still on a voluntary basis. And now that I've started to sell some of my paintings most of that money goes to them as well—I don't need it.'

'But you work in that shop—the one that sells the ridiculous dresses that look like the inner tubes of tyres!'

She shook her head. 'No. I don't. The WAO office is directly above that. Stark Designs lets us have it for next to nothing, providing that one of us covers their staff breaks.'

'But why didn't you tell me any of this before?' he queried.

'Oh, Liam—come *on*! You marched back into my life and carried me off—quite literally. I didn't think you were interested in *me*. I was supposed to be just doing you a favour in return for you getting off my stepfather's back.'

'But earlier you said you don't care what happens to him.'

'No,' she said, very quietly. 'I don't. I never did. Not really.'

He frowned. 'Then why did you agree to come?'

This was slightly more tricky. If he knew how she really felt about him, he might feel guilty. In fact, she had a funny feeling that if he *did* realise she was still in love with him, he actually might *not* take her to bed. He struck her as the kind of man who might consider that to be taking advantage . . . And, while she might morally applaud that kind of attitude, she had decided that she wanted one more night with Liam—and one more night she was determined to have. So it was imperative that he *didn't* find out.

'Why?' he repeated. 'Why did you agree to come?'

She gave the kind of nonchalant small shrug which should have won her an Oscar. 'Feminine curiosity,' she confided. 'Show me a woman in the world who says she wouldn't take the opportunity to suss out her ex-husband's lifestyle—and I'll show you a liar.'

'I see,' he said thoughtfully. 'Hmm. And what do you think of your er—ex-husband's lifestyle?'

Would describing it as the Garden of Eden be a bit over the top? she wondered. Something of a giveaway, in any case! 'It's—er—very nice,' she said lamely.

'Is it?' he murmured, and she could hear a smile in his voice. He shifted his long legs and put his arm around her shoulder, pulling her close to him.

At last! Scarlett nestled against him like a chick in the nest.

'And before that?'

She sighed. 'Before what?'

'Before your conscience got the better of you and you went abroad. All those photographs of you— with all those men. I suppose you were just doing research for some social documentary, were you?'

She sat up in indignation. 'Well, you can jolly take that abrasive, *accusing* tone out of your voice! If you must know it was a drag! It bored me rigid! I did it because it filled up the days—and I needed something to do that, because—'

'Because?'

She glared at him. 'Because I happened to be missing you like hell, if you must know!'

He let out a long sigh.

'But of course I soon got over *that*,' she interposed hastily.

'Of course,' he echoed gravely. 'Interesting.'

'Interesting! Oh, for God's sake, Liam Rouse—why don't you bloody well kiss me?'

'I thought you'd never ask,' he chuckled, and pulled her down so that she was lying on his lap. He stared down into her face for a long time, but his face was still remarkably serious. She could still read a question in his eyes.

'Now what is it?' Scarlett sighed, but it was a gentle, sad sigh, because in her heart she knew what was coming.

'I just want you to tell me one thing. I need to know *why*, Scarlett. Why you lied to me about the baby. Because lying was so out of character for you. Was it really just to get me to marry you?'

'You wouldn't have married me if there hadn't been a baby, would you?'

He was silent for a moment, then he shook his head. 'No,' he said honestly. 'Not at that time. Oh, I had decided to marry you some day—but not until I had finished university.'

Diplomatic of him to say that. 'I thought not. That's probably why it happened.'

His eyes narrowed. 'Why *what* happened?'

She moved away from him and twisted her hands around in her lap. She'd told no one, not a soul—apart from the doctor who had counselled her much later. Did she have the courage to tell Liam?

'Sweetheart—what?'

It was the gentle tone that did it; perhaps she was being blinded by the softness in that warm, blue stare, but Liam, of all the people in the world, deserved to know.

'I didn't lie to you about the pregnancy, but there was no pregnancy.'

'You're not making sense.'

She sighed. 'It didn't make a lot of sense to me at the time. I *did* miss three periods, my breasts *were* aching and I felt nauseated in the mornings. And we *had* had unprotected sex. But I was too frightened to go to the doctor.'

'I know,' he said gently. 'I was there—remember?'

'It was what they call a phantom pregnancy,' said Scarlett bluntly. 'All the physical manifestations of expecting a baby, which my body had manufactured. Probably because I secretly yearned to have your baby, and because I knew that that would tie you to me.' Her voice quivered a little as she strove to be matter-of-fact about it. 'Apparently, it's a kind of hysterical reaction—and it happens more among young girls...'

'Scarlett. *Scarlett*. Darling.' And he gathered her close again and she fell into his embrace, let him hold her and rock her, her eyes closed with relief, until he pushed her away, still holding her, so that he could look into her eyes. 'Why in heaven's name didn't you tell me?'

'Oh, *Liam*! How could I? Because when I discovered that I *wasn't* pregnant it seemed the perfect let-out clause for you,' she said quietly. 'Don't you see? I *had* trapped you into marriage—a marriage that you didn't really want or need. It was so ill-timed—disastrously timed, really—in terms of your career and what you wanted to do with your life.'

He nodded his head. 'Why didn't you come to see me when you got my letter? Why did you send Humphrey?'

'I was in a state of shock. You'd gone, and there was to be no baby. I felt . . .' She hesitated, before confronting him with the brutal truth. 'I felt as though the bottom had dropped out of my world. Humphrey persuaded me that it would be better if an independent person went to try and sort things out.'

'*Independent*!' he snarled. 'Hah! You know that he offered me money, don't you?'

Scarlett's eyes widened in disbelieving horror. 'He didn't!'

He nodded grimly. 'Oh, yes. He told me that you wanted out, and he asked me what it would take to keep me out of your life for good. Said he was prepared to be very generous. He actually appealed to my better nature and suggested that if I really loved you, as I claimed, I would see it wasn't fair to stay married to you.' Here he gave a kind of grimace. 'Not when you could do so much *better* for yourself.'

'But why did you listen to him?'

He lifted both her hands to his mouth, gently kissing each one before gazing into her eyes with a candid blue stare. 'Because I thought that there might be some truth in what he said. At the time

I had nothing—no prospects, nothing. I thought of the way we'd been living, how poor we'd been, and then I thought of the choices—either more of the same or accepting Humphrey's help. I thought that you were probably regretting ever getting married— and that maybe you *could* do better for yourself. So I told Humphrey exactly where he could shove his money, and he left.'

'No wonder you hate him. Especially after what he did to your mother.'

He shook his head. 'I don't hate him, Scarlett. I pity him. He lives life on a different level—a worthless and superficial level.' He traced a blue vein which ran like a tributary over the pale river of her wrist. 'Then, when I saw all your clubbing photos, I thought that perhaps I had made the right decision after all.'

'Oh, God,' she said sadly. 'What a stupid, stupid mix-up. Liam! What are you doing?'

He was pulling her to her feet, an irrepressible grin all over his face. 'I sort of got the idea,' he said solemnly, 'that you wanted to take advantage of my body. So I'm giving you permission to do exactly that!' And he put his arm around her shoulder and walked her towards what was obviously the door of his bedroom.

Scarlett gave a shudder which was a mixture of excitement and trepidation. Strange how she had been wanting this for so long and yet now felt oddly shy.

He pushed the door open, and, his arms still around her, led her inside.

The first thing she saw was the window.

'But it *doesn't* look out over the city!' she squealed in delight. Instead there was the endless, shimmering blue expanse of the Indian Ocean.

He frowned down at her in confusion. 'What?'

'The view from your window! It doesn't have a panoramic view of the city!'

'I'm still not clear what—'

'Kelly told me it had! And it hasn't. So obviously she hasn't been in here...'

He took hold of her shoulders and stared down at her fiercely. 'Of course she hasn't been in here! Just because I happen to know a woman it doesn't mean that I've been to bed with her. In fact...'

'What?'

He shook his head. 'It doesn't matter. Nothing matters in the world at this moment, Scarlett, other than you kissing me. Because if you don't—'

His words were halted by the simple expedient of Scarlett standing on tiptoe and reaching up to kiss him.

It was the most wonderful kiss—tender yet passionate—and emotion welled up within her, so that she was actually afraid that she might burst into tears.

He drew back. 'Mmm. You're beautiful. Exquisite. Do you know that?'

'So are you!' she murmured shakily.

By now he had removed the emerald overshirt so that she was wearing just the white body and matching jeans. He ran his finger down over the smooth curve of her breast. 'Whoever designed

SHARON KENDRICK 173

these garments,' he grumbled, 'must have been a sadist. Think how long it's going to take to get you out of it.'

'Oh, I don't know,' she purred. 'You should see where it unbuttons.'

'Why don't you show me?' he suggested, and went to lie on the bed, his head resting back on his arms, his eyes half-hooded as he surveyed her.

She'd never done a striptease before. She kicked off her deck shoes and slithered out of her jeans, until she was wearing nothing but the snowy body which clung to every curve like a second skin. And then she got shy.

'Come here,' he said, as though he understood, and held his arms out, and she ran to the bed and into them. 'Want me to take the rest off?'

'Yes, please.'

His fingers skated down over her breasts, skimming over her stomach, and further, and deliciously down until he had located the three buttons. 'Mmm,' he said again. 'I take back everything I said.'

His fingers tantalised her as they barely touched her, when she so wanted to be touched. Scarlett felt one of the buttons snap open. Was he deliberately tormenting her by taking so long to do it? she wondered in a fever.

The second button snapped open. Scarlett felt she'd *die* if he didn't touch her soon.

The third button—at last! Scarlett gave a little cry of relief which fast became a little moan of pleasure as his fingers finally stroked at her with slow, tantalising little movements, and she melted into syrup all over him.

'On second thoughts,' he murmured, 'I can see that this is going to prove a very useful garment indeed. Just think, any time, anywhere...'

'Shut up,' she commanded, and pulled his head down to kiss him.

The kiss went on and on. Scarlett never wanted it to stop, but clearly Liam did.

'Take that thing off,' he said in an unsteady voice as he pulled at the belt of his jeans.

Sitting back on her heels, she peeled it off so that she was totally naked, seeing his eyes darken as they appraised the lush bloom of her body.

He was pulling at the buttons on his shirt, but his eyes seemed to be mesmerised by the thrust of her breasts, and he wasn't having very much success.

'Help me,' he ordered.

Well, two could play at this game of torture! Scarlett gave a cat's smile as she leaned over him and laid the palm of her hand on his lap, over what she could see was a very aroused and very sensitive area indeed. 'Like this?' she taunted softly, and moved her palm in a slowly provocative semi-circle.

'Witch,' he swore softly, and the shirt was ripped off and discarded. He pushed her hand away impatiently as he dealt with the zip, finally wriggling out of his jeans and his boxer shorts until he, too, was naked.

Scarlett licked her lips as she gazed in awe at him, magnificently and arrogantly aroused, and his eyes flared as he pushed her down onto the bed. He came to lie on top of her before kissing her again and again and again, until she squirmed in a frenzy beneath him.

'Want me now?' he muttered thickly. 'Do you, Scarlett?'

'Oh, yes! Oh, please, yes.'

She felt him move fractionally away to position himself for the final conquest, and she moved her hand up to run her hand lovingly through his hair.

Something in the movement stilled him, and to her incredulity he suddenly levered himself away from her to the end of the bed, where he knelt staring at her with blazing eyes.

'It's no good!' he grated. 'I can't do it! I'm sorry, Scarlett, but I can't make love to you!'

CHAPTER ELEVEN

SCARLETT stared at Liam in amazement. 'Wh-what did you say?'

'I said that I can't make love to you!'

She blinked, then sat up and reached her hand out to lay it on his muscular forearm. 'Liam,' she whispered, 'don't you think I'm nervous about this too?'

He looked at her and snorted. 'Nervous? Forgive me, Scarlett—perhaps I should have phrased it a little better. For "can't" read "won't".'

'Won't?' she echoed in confusion.

'That's right,' he said grimly.

'But why?'

'Just look at you!' he accused her. 'Just look at what you're wearing!'

She stared down at her naked body, now even more confused. 'But I'm not wearing anything!' she protested.

'Oh, really?' He grabbed her left hand and held it up in front of her face. 'What's this, then?'

'What? Liam, have you gone mad?'

'There you were, in my bed—'

'We were actually lying on top of it,' she said, but he silenced her with a look.

'Wearing nothing but that damned engagement ring! I'm sorry, Scarlett—but I'm not making love to you while you're wearing another man's ring!'

She smiled. 'Well, that's easily remedied!' And she slid it off and laid it down on the bedside locker. She looked up at him expectantly, but he was shaking his head, still with that same grim look on his face.

'I'm sorry, Scarlett—I think you've misunderstood.' And he got off the bed and began climbing back into his jeans. 'Whether or not you are actually wearing it is academic. It's the principle which lies behind it. I'm afraid that I can't make love to you while you are engaged to another man. So I'm afraid we're going to have to go back to England and you're going to have to tell Henry that it's over. *Then*, and only then can we start again.'

A gurgle of laughter bubbled against Scarlett's mouth, but she kept her face straight. 'You naturally assume that I'll tell Henry it's over?'

'You're too damned right I do! You're a one-woman man Scarlett—there's absolutely no doubt in my mind about that!'

Scarlett thrilled with delight. And there she'd been, thinking he'd changed. When he came out with possessive and ridiculously old-fashioned statements like that he was exactly the same as her old, passionate Liam, who had seen things in distinctly black and white terms.

'So you'd better get your clothes back on,' he ordered.

Scarlett reclined on his pillows like a vamp. 'I'm afraid that I can't do that, Liam,' she purred.

'Well, I'm not about to do it for you, if that's what you're hinting at!'

'I'm not. I mean that I can't go back to England and tell Henry that it's over...' And she cowered in thrilled horror as he marched over to the bed and picked her up bodily by the shoulders.

'*What*?' he thundered.

Well, she wasn't risking a second more of *that* kind of rage. 'I mean, I can't,' she amended hastily, 'because I've already done it. I've already broken off our engagement. I did it just before I flew out to Australia with you.'

'What?' He sat down on the bed with a start. 'Why?'

'Why, what?'

'You always damned well say "Why, what?"'!' he exploded. 'Why did you break your engagement off?'

Careful, Scarlett—don't give too much away. 'Because I thought—er—because I had an idea that—this—might happen.'

The suspicious look hadn't yet left his eyes. 'So how come you're still wearing his ring?' he demanded.

'*Because*,' she said patiently, 'you did bring me here in rather a hurry, if you recall. I didn't have time to take it to a bank, and I certainly haven't got a safe in my flat. I was afraid that it might get stolen, and so I decided that the safest way to look after it would be to actually wear it—until I could give it back.'

He stood looking at her for a minute, then at the ring, then back to Scarlett. Then he grinned.

'Hell!' he exclaimed softly, and then he picked the ring up, strode over to the open window, and hurled it as hard as he could out into the sky.

Scarlett watched in horror as it curved in a glittering arc before dropping down, heaven only knew where.

'What the hell did you do that for?' she cried.

'Because I want it to join your short-lived engagement—consigned to oblivion!'

'But it cost an absolute fortune!'

'Don't worry—I'll replace it. Or pay for it.' And he turned back to the bed, still grinning.

But Scarlett needed to know something. 'Liam?'

'Mmm?'

'Why did it bother you so much—me wearing another man's ring?'

He gave her a look of pure exasperation. 'Because there's only one ring you'll wear on that finger—and it'll be mine!'

Which didn't really sound like a 'no strings' affair at all, did it? 'You mean that this is going to be—permanent?' she ventured.

'Of course it's going to be permanent—what the hell did you think it was going to be? I love you, woman! I love you to death—I always have. And sooner or later you're going to climb down off your high-horse and admit that you love me too!'

Scarlett's eyes widened into saucers. 'You love me?' she queried.

Liam nodded.

'What, even then—when we were first together?'

'Especially then,' he said gently. 'But even more now.'

'But you never *once* told me so!' she accused him. 'Why ever not?'

His smile was rueful. 'For reasons possibly too complex to analyse. I was certain that your so-called love for me was nothing more than a passing fancy. I was always waiting for you to change your mind. I imagine that I somehow thought if you knew about my *real* feelings for you it would give you an added burden of guilt if you should change your mind and want to leave me.'

There was still something she didn't understand. 'But you were going to let me walk out of your life tomorrow—back to England.'

He shook his head. 'Back to England, yes. Out of my life—no. I decided that if you really wanted to go home then I wasn't going to coerce you to stay any more. But I was planning on coming with you. I suddenly realised that I didn't need to isolate you miles from anywhere to win you back. I knew,' he concluded, with an arrogance which appalled and yet thrilled her, 'that I could do that anywhere.'

'Oh, I do love you, Liam,' she whispered fervently. 'Really, I do.'

She would treasure the look on his face for the rest of her life, but he wasn't going to get off *that* easily for chucking several thousand pounds' worth of diamond ring out of the window.

She wriggled off the bed and began walking towards the door, and he stared at her in amazement.

'Now where do you think you're going?'

She gave him a look of wide-eyed innocence. 'But you told me to get my clothes on. You did, Liam. You honestly did—'

With a roar he was upon her. She hit the plush carpet with a gentle thud as he landed on top of her, and they lay together—a tangle of limbs.

'Oh, Liam,' she whispered, revelling in the freedom to speak the words she'd suppressed for so long. 'I love you.'

'Then why don't you show me?' he growled softly, but there was a break to his voice.

'Hello, sweetheart.'

'You're late,' smiled Scarlett as Liam walked in.

They'd been in London for a week, and had been staying at the Ritz in London while they waited for the necessary paperwork on Scarlett's permanent visa into Australia to be completed.

The day before they had been to see Scarlett's bemused solicitor, Frances, to tell her that the decree absolute on their divorce would now be redundant.

Frances had let her eyes run briefly over Liam's tall and rangy frame. 'I can see why,' she had observed drily.

Liam came over to the chair where Scarlett had been sitting reading, and gave her a long, luxurious kiss.

'Mmm. I needed that.' He sat down in the chair next to her. 'It's been a *long* day.'

She got to her feet. 'Need a drink?'

'I need *you*,' he said firmly. 'Come here.' And he pulled her down onto his lap.

'Did you see Henry?'

'I did.'

'And what did he say?'

'Any irritation he might have been feeling quickly vanished when I told him I'd reimburse him for the ring.' He smiled. 'He just about doubled what it was worth, but I let him. I could afford to be magnanimous. After all, I got the girl in the end.'

'Was he—er—*very* upset?'

Liam looked at her from out of the corner of his eye. 'Want the true version?' he quizzed.

'Of course I do!'

'Well, when I mentioned that you'd given all your fortune away to a charity organisation he went slightly green. And when I compounded that by hinting that Humphrey's business wasn't all that it should be he looked rather relieved. I think, my darling, that your Henry is something of an old-fashioned fortune-hunter.' He frowned at her. 'You don't have to answer this—but one thing I haven't been able to understand is...well, why Henry, exactly?'

Scarlett ran her fingers through his thick, dark hair and sighed. 'I was twenty-eight and I knew I'd never fall in love again—not after you. But Henry didn't seem to want love. It was to be an old-fashioned merger of two families, and he convinced me that it could work. Of course, if it was my supposed fortune he was after I can imagine how pleased he was that I've called it off. But seriously, Liam—' and her eyes softened as she looked down at him '—a lot of people settle for marriages like that. Steady, undemanding—'

'A nightmare,' he cut in. 'And as unlike ours as you could imagine.'

'I know.' She smiled happily, then frowned remorsefully. 'Poor Henry.'

'Maybe not.' He smiled too. 'The last thing I heard was that he's been romancing your friend Camilla.'

Scarlett giggled. 'Camilla's as rich as hell—*and* she's desperate for a man.'

'There you go, then!'

'And Humphrey? Did you go to see him?'

He nodded. 'I did. I told him that I won't press to have his loans repaid immediately—but that repaid they must be. He actually had the grace to admit that he'd had his suspicions that I was behind the buying up of his assets.'

'And *that's* why he tried to rush my wedding to Henry through?' Scarlett hazarded.

'Exactly,' agreed Liam grimly. 'I saw your mother too. Told her we'd visit them next week, when they've had a bit of time to get used to the idea that we're back together. I also told them that they will be very welcome to visit us in Australia.'

Scarlett flung her arms around his neck. 'Oh, Liam,' she whispered. 'Did you really?'

'Of course I did. No matter what's gone on in the past they *are* family—and I treat them accordingly.'

'You are sweet.'

'Scarlett, I am *not* sweet!' he said sternly. 'I just happen to be a soft touch where you're concerned. Now, one other thing.' And he fished around in his pocket and withdrew a small box.

'What's that?'

He smiled. 'I remember you telling Kelly how I couldn't afford to buy you a ring the first time around. So I'm making amends. Here.'

It was a square-cut and brilliant topaz, surrounded by tiny glittering diamonds.

'Oh, Liam,' she breathed. 'It's exquisite. And different. And absolutely gorgeous.'

'Just like me!'

'You are the most arrogant man in the world!'

He smiled. 'And don't you just love it? Here. Let me put it on.'

And naturally it fitted perfectly.

'I thought that the gold was the exact colour of your eyes,' he said thoughtfully.

'Oh, Liam!'

His eyes twinkled. 'You seem to spend an awful lot of time lately saying "Oh, Liam!".'

She kissed him. 'I know. Crazy, isn't it?'

'If that's crazy, then I love it,' he murmured softly. 'Are you hungry?'

'Starving!'

'Want to eat in or out?'

She traced the curving line of his mouth with her forefinger. 'Don't mind.'

'On second thoughts...' he ran an idle finger down over one silk-covered breast '...dinner's a moveable feast, isn't it?' And he kissed her.

But he didn't carry on making love to her. Instead he tipped her face up to stare at him, and his own expression was suddenly very serious. 'There's something I want you to know, Scarlett. That there isn't anyone who could possibly know what the view is like from my bedroom window.' He paused. 'Except you.'

She gazed at him uncomprehendingly before it clicked, and her heart leapt. 'You mean—?'

'There was no one else for me. Ever. You're the only woman. You always have been, and you always will be.' He pulled her close. 'Everything I did, I did for you. I was determined to succeed, but it was all for you.'

'You mean that you actually *planned* to come back for me?'

He looked at her in exasperation. 'Of course I did! I just didn't plan to take so long to do it. And then, when you damned well got engaged, I realised that I needed to act quickly.'

'You certainly did that,' she whispered, and then clapped her hand over her mouth. 'Your business deal!' she exclaimed. 'When I was supposed to play hostess for you! Oh, Liam,' she said worriedly, 'will it all fall through?'

The blue eyes glinted. 'I have to confess, sweetheart, that the whole so-called deal was a complete fabrication to lure you away.'

'*You*,' she said firmly, 'are completely unscrupulous.'

'Mmm. 'Fraid so.' He stared into her face, and she felt her heart begin to quicken. 'I want to make one thing clear, Scarlett,' he said sternly. 'This is a new beginning for us. I want to start all over again. Beginning next week. How does the idea of going to Bali for a month grab you?'

'Bali?' she squeaked. 'What for?'

'A honeymoon. *Our* honeymoon—too long delayed.' His voice lowered to a velvet embrace. 'I love you, Scarlett—more than words can ever say.'

Her whole life with Liam, she suspected dreamily, was going to be one long honeymoon—but his ego was quite healthy enough already, without her telling him that. 'And I love you too, Liam—but now will you please shut up and kiss me?'

'Oh, Scarlett,' he murmured. 'What *am* I going to do with you?'

She slanted him a look which spoke volumes. 'Oh, don't worry, my darling,' she whispered, her hands sliding right down his chest. 'I'm sure we'll think of something!'

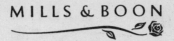

GET 4 BOOKS
AND A MYSTERY GIFT

Return this coupon and we'll send you 4 Mills & Boon Romances and a mystery gift absolutely FREE! We'll even pay the postage and packing for you.

We're making you this offer to introduce you to the benefits of Reader Service: FREE home delivery of brand-new Mills & Boon Romances, at least a month before they are available in the shops, FREE gifts and a monthly Newsletter packed with information.

Accepting these FREE books and gift places you under no obligation to buy, you may cancel at any time, even after receiving just your free shipment. Simply complete the coupon below and send it to:

MILLS & BOON READER SERVICE, FREEPOST, CROYDON, SURREY, CR9 3WZ.

No stamp needed

Yes, please send me 4 free Mills & Boon Romances and a mystery gift. I understand that unless you hear from me, I will receive 6 superb new titles every month for just £2.10* each postage and packing free. I am under no obligation to purchase any books and I may cancel or suspend my subscription at any time, but the free books and gifts will be mine to keep in any case. (I am over 18 years of age)

1EP6R

Ms/Mrs/Miss/Mr _____

Address _____

_____

_____ Postcode _____

mps MAILING PREFERENCE SERVICE

DMA

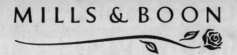

Next Month's Romances

Each month you can choose from a wide variety of romance with Mills & Boon. Below are the new titles to look out for next month.

ONLY BY CHANCE	Betty Neels
THE MORNING AFTER	Michelle Reid
THE DESERT BRIDE	Lynne Graham
THE RIGHT CHOICE	Catherine George
FOR THE LOVE OF EMMA	Lucy Gordon
WORKING GIRL	Jessica Hart
THE LADY'S MAN	Stephanie Howard
THE BABY BUSINESS	Rebecca Winters
WHITE LIES	Sara Wood
THAT MAN CALLAHAN!	Catherine Spencer
FLIRTING WITH DANGER	Kate Walker
THE BRIDE'S DAUGHTER	Rosemary Gibson
SUBSTITUTE ENGAGEMENT	Jayne Bauling
NOT PART OF THE BARGAIN	Susan Fox
THE PERFECT MAN	Angela Devine
JINXED	Day Leclaire

Available from WH Smith, John Menzies, Volume One, Forbuoys, Martins, Woolworths, Tesco, Asda, Safeway and other paperback stockists.